Wickedness

Wickedness

Deborah White

A TEMPLAR BOOK

First published in the UK in 2011 by Templar Publishing,
an imprint of The Templar Company Limited,
The Granary, North Street, Dorking, Surrey, RH4 1DN, UK
www.templarco.co.uk

ISBN 978-1-84877-531-2

Printed by CPI Mackays, Chatham, Kent

For Al and Nik, with love

The Prophecy

He who loves wickedness
Cloaks himself in the odour of sanctity.
At his coming will be great plagues.

He seeks the one who holds the key to life,
The true daughter and the red-haired maiden.

When she is found, then all will hear
Thoth's mighty voice
And the wicked shall be made small as dust
Before the storm.

Chapter 1

It was the funeral that afternoon. People would be coming back to the house after the burial. A few old friends. A couple of distant cousins. No religious service though. Grandma hadn't believed in any of that.

"If there is a God, Claire," she'd said, "then he isn't in the churches. He doesn't speak through them. No, when you find wickedness in this world, don't look to anyone else to save you from it. You have only yourself."

Now she was dead and Claire was sent running upstairs to fetch chairs. People would need somewhere to sit as they sipped their drinks and ate their sandwiches. As they laughed too loudly, saying what a shame it always took a death to bring them together like this.

She found a bentwood chair on the landing. It was light as a feather, so she took that down first.

"Any more?" said Claire's mum, sounding fussed and distracted. Looking tired, and puffy-eyed. "Try Grandma's bedroom."

She didn't hear Claire's sharp intake of breath. Had no time anyway for a daughter who might not want to go into the room where Grandma had died just a week before.

"Hurry!"

So there she was, standing outside Grandma's bedroom door, feeling unsteady and afraid. She had to take a deep breath before she could turn the brass knob and push open the door into the wide silence of the room.

Heavy lace curtains filtered only a very little light through the bay of the window, but Claire could still see, just.

There was the big bed, so high off the ground that Grandma had needed a stool to climb in. A chest of drawers to one side, at the right height for a mirror. A small clock, still ticking. A hairbrush, strands of Grandma's long dark hair caught in it. A pillbox. A jewellery case, already lightly covered with a talcum of dust. And on the other side of the bed, a heavy looking carved oak chair with Grandma's silk dressing gown still tumbled over it.

"Claire! What are you doing? I need those chairs now, not next week!"

"Coming! I'm coming!" She hurried to pick up the dressing gown, breathing in as she did, an echo of the sharp smell that was Grandma. And it was then that she uncovered it. An emerald-green box, resting on the seat of the chair and shimmering softly in the half light.

She dropped the dressing gown onto the bed, then hunkered down on her heels so she could get a better look. It wasn't very big. As long as her hand, and a hand's length deep. And when she plucked up the courage to touch it, it was as smooth as glass under her fingers.

It was unexpectedly light. It almost seemed to float in her hands. She turned it this way and that, looking to see if there was any clue as to what it might be. There was nothing. It wasn't decorated at all, except for a faint line marking the edge of the lid. She looked closer. There was an oval etched deep in black, just at the place you'd expect a keyhole to be. And etched inside the oval, a crocodile's head resting on the palm of an outstretched hand. She knew at once that it was some sort of hieroglyph. She'd seen writing just like it at the museum.

"Claire! Hurry up will you?"

Giving the box one last look and quite forgetting about taking the chair, she tumbled down the stairs, breathless, thinking, *I'll ask Mum about it later. When everyone's gone. Maybe she'll know what it is.*

But maybe she wouldn't ask, because Claire's dad had come to the funeral. Uninvited. Looking like a stranger in his charcoal-grey suit and black tie. And her mum had got very emotional when he'd said, "Let me take them back home, Jill. Give you some space."

Them being Claire and her little sister Michaela. Micky for short.

"Space," she'd shouted at him, loud enough for everyone to hear. A split-second's uncomfortable silence, then a crescendo of embarrassed chatter. "I thought you were the one who needed that… to, what was it… find out who you really are?" Her face was drained of colour. Her hands clenched so tight her knuckles showed white. "Well I know *what* you are. You're weak and selfish. No, you can't have them. Their home's here, in their grandmother's house. It's my house now and they're staying."

Manuscript 1

My name is Margrat Jennet. I live in the house of Nicholas Robert Benedict, physician. For my mother and father are both dead and I fear, now, for my own life. But I do not think he means to harm me – yet. For I make him think there is still hope of a daughter, a precious girl child.

When he presses close. When I feel the warmth of his breath sweet on my cheek. When I feel the heat of his body, and see the tremor of pulse in his neck, I do not move away. My heart beats very fast. I feel a prickle of fear raise the hairs on the nape of my neck.

"Ah, Margrat," he says. "You smell of the sweet meadow hay."

And I tremble like the harvest mouse in hiding, as the swish, swish, swish of the scythe draws near.

He said that my mother made him my guardian. Certainly I did see a will, made after my father's death.

It was in my mother's hand, and bore her true signature. It may have been that she was forced to sign. But I think she did so in good faith. For who would not trust such a man? He is known everywhere. In high, and in low places. And he is fine and handsome. Tall, and smooth-skinned. He has dark eyes burning like coals. The hot, restless smell of him when he is close makes me afraid, yet draws me in. Like a moth to the candle's flame.

These thoughts shame me. I am tested every minute of every day, and may fail to hold out against him. So I have vowed to write down everything I know and place it somewhere safe, so that, God willing, any who come after me will be forewarned and may be saved.

Chapter 2

Later, in the bedroom Claire was having to share with Micky – when it was dark, and the only sounds were the sharp cracks and creaks of an old house settling, the soft shallow whispering sound of Micky breathing – Claire thought about what her mother had said. My house. They're staying. Typical. Everything always revolved around what her mum wanted.

Claire's own breathing quickened. She wanted her mum and dad to sort out their lives, so that she could get on with hers. She wanted to be lying in her own bed, in her own room, in her old house. She wanted to be kept awake at night worrying about those things that her mum and dad would think were trivial and unimportant. Friendships: Katrin and Jade. Jade, who had three tattoos and her nose, eyebrow and belly button pierced. Katrin who didn't and never would. Because Katrin was going places and already knew that, where she wanted to go, appearances mattered. That most people don't take the time or trouble to see what's swimming below the surface. That acting the part is, most of the time, all that you need to do.

And Claire. Not knowing how she fitted in. Anywhere. Being afraid she would be the sort of person who had the tattoo and piercing, but only where it didn't show. Being afraid because she hadn't felt anything when Grandma had died. Nothing at all. And that wasn't right was it? Only to feel relief, because she hadn't liked her. Had been scared of her even. Had found her fierce intelligence, dark moods and oppressive silences unsettling.

Claire sat up. Threw back the covers. The cold chill of the room hit her like a wave. She swung her legs over the side of the bed. Felt panic closing her throat and beads of sweat forming at her hairline. And all the while dispassionately observing her own terror.

"Micky?"

But Micky didn't wake.

Claire crawled into Micky's bed. Rolled Micky

onto her side to make room. Folded her body round Micky's, needing to breathe in, just this once, the soft, sour, familiar smell of her skin, her hair. Felt the brittle, chicken-winged boniness of her and clung tight.

Manuscript 2

It began ten months before my 14th birthday. On the 27th day of February, 1665. In weather so cruel and bitterly cold, birds fell clear out of the sky, and a boy was found frozen to death, just a step away, in Jerusalem Alley. But I gave no thought to that. The river was iced so thick that a frost fair was set out upon it. I'd heard there were any number of stalls and entertainments and I wanted to go.

My father had given me a little money for some work I had done for him in his shop; unpacking a leather bag that had recently come into his possession, and was full of scrolls covered in strange writing. Not letters, but pictures used as signs. My father had said they were hieroglyphics, the language of the Ancient Egyptians. And there was no one still alive who could understand it, but there were many who tried.

"For it was believed, Margrat," my father leaned

in close to me. His voice fell to a whisper, "that the Egyptians knew many wondrous secrets and anyone able to decipher their language would be privy to them. How powerful and rich they would be then."

Oh! I determined at once that I would be the one to unlock those secrets. How happy my mother would be with me if I could. For we would be rich. Have wealth enough for her to forgive me the sin of being born with red hair. But until then I meant to spend the money that I did have as quick as I could, before my mother took it from me.

And that is how I first met with Doctor Nicholas Robert Benedict.

∞∞∞∞

I had been at the fair a long while, for there was plenty to see. I'd watched a puppet show, a rope-walker and the horse and carriage races. I'd bought a new ribbon and some lace to trim my dress. I'd paid my pennies to an old woman in a fortune-teller's booth. She took my money, read my palm, and told me she could see nothing but blackness. Which made me very cross, for that is no future at all. And so I stepped out of the booth in such a temper, I slipped on the ice and the shock of it took my breath clean away. My ankle turned under me and I would have fallen, but a man sprang forward and caught me. He held me tight in a clasp as hard as iron. I looked up into his eyes, deep and black as the night sky with no stars to light it.

Then I heard him say, "Margrat!"

"Do I know you, sir?" I asked, pulling back. There was something familiar about the smell of him and it disturbed me.

He smiled, and I noticed that his teeth were not rotten and black at all, but very white and even. His breath did not smell of decay, as most people's did, but was as sweet as honey.

"I saw you in your father's shop when I was enquiring after Egyptian scrolls," he said. "You seemed in a hurry then too. You pushed so close past me as I came in at the door, that a strand of your hair caught in the pin on my cloak. It was such a perfect red gold, that I took it for an omen of good fortune and kept it."

Then, before I had a moment to reflect on that, he told me his name.

I gasped and felt a hot flush flood my face. For this was the man all London seemed in awe of. His name spoken in excited whispers: Doctor Nicholas Benedict! Have you heard? He performs miracles and cures the sick! He is more wealthy than Croesus. Has more charms than the Devil himself. And, can you believe it, no wife to care for him.

Now he was asking if he might take me home, as his carriage was waiting nearby. Oh! Such moments are what fate turns on. I felt it, as if the world had stopped spinning for a heartbeat and I had stepped clean out of time.

He moved in close and took my arm. "Come, there is nothing to be afraid of."

Which seemed true, for it was said that he was always at Court and was a close friend of the King. Besides, my house was not far away, and the streets were full of people.

And he was such a fine, well-dressed gentleman. He wore a hat made of beaver fur trimmed with an ostrich feather. He carried a black lacquered cane, with a snake's head in silver and on his finger was a diamond ring.

I had met with many men of quality in my father's shop, behind St Paul's, where he dealt in rare books and manuscripts. But I had met no man before this, of whom all London seemed in awe.

So with my ankle beginning to swell and painful to walk on, I thanked him. Let him lift me up into the carriage. Sit so close to me, that I could feel the heat *from his body, and smell the sweet spiciness of his perfume. And though he spoke softly to me, I was struck quite dumb. My tongue tied into a thousand knots, and I was never in all my life so pleased to reach home.*

⋰ஓ௮ ஓ௮⋰

Our maid Jane came to the door and her mouth dropped open at the sight of me, Margrat Jennet, brought home in such a fine carriage.

The Doctor jumped out, then reached up to help me down. I felt his hands circle my waist inside my cloak. I felt his diamond ring pricking my side, and his thumbs pressing hard into my ribs as he lifted me out. My face came level with his. He drew in his breath and must have drawn mine in with it, for I had none left. And the world lost all its colour, and I was falling down.

When I awoke at last, it was to candle and firelight. The sound of coals hissing and shifting in the grate. Jane asleep on the truckle at the end of my bed. My hair loose and damp with sweat, spread out, my father said, like rays of the sun. Then other voices, and the door opening and my mother taking my hand and whispering excitedly in my ear, "Doctor Nicholas Benedict, no less. In my house, and tending to the

*health of my daughter! Be nice to him, my poppet,
won't you?"*

Even my father seemed amazed and grateful for it.

*"It was a lucky day you met with the Doctor,
Margrat. For he is just lately returned from Egypt, and
without his help you would have been lost. For you
were sick to your very soul, he said, and tied to this
world only by a thread. But by some magic he learned
on his travels, he brought you back to us."*

*My father turned, smiled, and held out his hand.
"Now he has come to see if you are feeling better." And
the Doctor stepped forward out of the shadows.*

I struggled to sit upright, but I was weak.

*"Shh. Be calm. Lie still now." The Doctor leaned
in so close over me that I could see how the pulse in his
neck quickened. How tiny prickles of sweat formed on
his forehead and upper lip. Like hot breath on a cold
windowpane.*

*Lightly stroking my hair back from my forehead, he
said, "The fever is not yet gone." Then he loosened the
ribbons around the neck of my nightgown, and the tips
of his fingers brushed the length of my collarbone.*

*Now he saw the ring on the braid about my neck,
and I thought all was undone. For I had stolen the
ring. Taken it from a leather bag full of scrolls I had*

unpacked for my father just a few days before. It had been tied on a thin braid of woven red linen. Not a beautiful ring, studded with precious jewels, but fashioned in plain gold, inset with an oval blue stone. The stone was carved with a crocodile's head resting upon the palm of an outstretched hand. It was unlike anything I had ever seen before.

I had tried it on at once, but it was so small it would not pass over the first joint on the ring finger of either hand, though I pushed and pushed. My hands are not dainty like my mother's.

At least, I thought, it will fit snug on my little finger, but it was too loose. Even so I meant to have it. But I knew that even if my father would let me keep it, my mother would not. If she thought it had worth, she would make my father sell it. So I had tied the ring on its braid around my neck.

I ought not to have taken it. I know that. But I liked the feel of it, resting warm and heavy against my skin.

How heavy it felt now, and hot. As if it were burning deep into my flesh. I looked up into the Doctor's eyes. Saw myself reflected small in them. Then, leaning in towards me, his mouth close to my ear, he whispered something so strange I felt a quiver of fear flood through me.

"Tell no one about the ring, Margrat. And do not wear it on your finger on pain of death. But keep it on its braid around your neck always, for its hieroglyphics protect you from Sekhmet. Her messengers, carrying pestilence, are even now spreading out through the lanes and alleyways of London. For the hour is near, and I must keep you safe. I have need of you, Margrat."

Chapter 3

The next morning, Micky had kicked and elbowed Claire out of a deep sleep. And she'd had another bad dream, though she couldn't remember this one. Just the dark, whispy threads of it still tangling in her head.

"Get out. Out!" And with one push Claire was on the floor.

"What did you do that for?"

Micky stuck her tongue out, then pulled the duvet over her head and curled up into a ball. "Go away!"

Claire sighed, no use getting cross. Micky was angry and missing their old life too. She picked herself up and went and showered. Washed and dried her hair, got dressed and was halfway down the stairs, when she saw her mum.

"Oh, Claire, I nearly forgot. I found an envelope on Grandma's desk. It had your name on it. I put it on the dresser in front of the big blue plate." She said this over her shoulder as she was leaving to go and collect more things from their old house. "And look after Micky for me. I won't be long."

She slammed the door behind her with such force that Claire could feel the shudder through the soles of her bare feet. On and up until she could feel its buzz in her jawbone, and all the tiny bones in her skull.

* * *

It was an ordinary brown envelope, innocently resting against the blue Spode plate. Her name and 'To be opened only in the event of my death' written on it in Grandma's thick italic script. She took it off the shelf. Whatever was inside was unexpectedly heavy. It slid the length of the envelope, and in surprise Claire let it slip out of her grasp. It fell to the floor with a clink. What could it be? A watch maybe, a bracelet, a ring? She bent and picked up the envelope and tore it open. Pulled out a sheaf of yellowing papers tied up with a red linen braid. And something else.

She tipped the contents into the palm of her hand. A ring then, gold and set with a blue stone.

It felt warm and heavy; was luminous against her skin.

Taking a closer look, she saw it was carved with exactly the same hieroglyphs as on the box in Grandma's room. She tried it on the ring finger of her right hand. Too big. She had small hands. But it fitted perfectly on the middle finger.

The same sign as on the box, and it looked like it was the same shape and size too. Except, the carving on the ring was raised, and the one on the box was indented. As if the one would fit into the other. Just like a key fits into the barrel of a lock.

But underlying her excitement, was the sharply metallic taste of fear, which was stupid, because what was there to be afraid of? Nothing.

So leaving the envelope and the sheaf of papers on the table, she went out of the kitchen and took the stairs slowly. She took measured steps along the landing to Grandma's room, took one last deep breath, opened the door and went straight to the chair, in its place by the bed. And there was the box, on the seat, half covered over again by Grandma's dressing gown, which was as cool and soft pink as second skin.

Claire knelt in front of the chair. Lifted aside

the dressing gown. Pressed the ring into the oval cartouche on the box. And it fitted exactly. Yes!

But the box didn't magically open. Nothing happened at all. Except... She turned her head sharply. Caught the whisper of a scent; musty, acrid, sweet, seductive. And thought she could hear someone calling out her name. So convincing and compelling that she called out, "Yes? What is it?" her heart leaping up into her mouth as she waited for the reply.

But there were no footsteps, there was no rustle of clothing, no answering voice. Only the soft tick, tick, tick of the bedside clock. And the distant sounds of life out on the street. A car. The nasal drone of a milk float. A dog barking. Familiar. Soothing.

Stupid, she thought. *You are so stupid.* What did she think was going to happen? It was just a box and an old ring. That was all. It was a puzzle though. Why had Grandma left them for her?

She was looking down at her hand, still wearing the ring, when she heard the car pull up outside. The slam, slam of the car door. Shouting. The rattle of the front door opening.

"Claire, I'm back! Come and give me a hand to

unload, will you? I've got bags of stuff in the car."

Claire jumped up, guiltily, as if she'd been caught doing something wicked. Her first thought was to slip the ring off her finger and hide it. She didn't want her mum seeing it, because she'd want to try it on, and then if she liked it, she'd want to keep it. She was like that. Acquisitive.

But the ring wouldn't come off. It was gripping her finger too tightly. Now someone was running up the stairs and skipping along the landing. Micky.

Panicking, Claire was pulling so hard on the ring, she thought she'd dislocate her finger.

"What are you doing in here?" Micky was standing in the door now. But Claire knew she wouldn't step into Grandma's bedroom. She was too scared.

Claire quickly pulled the sleeve of her sweatshirt down over her hand and pushed past her out of the door. "Just proving there's nothing to be afraid of," she said, turning to look Micky straight in the eye. "Because there isn't. It's just a room someone died in. Grandma's not still there you know."

"I know that stupid," Micky said, kick, kick,

kicking the toe of her trainer against the door frame. "It's just that…"

"What?" But she knew what Micky was thinking, because she was feeling it too. Pressure. Panic. Fear. Irrational and stupid because there was nothing to fear.

Micky looked so anxious and forlorn, Claire wanted to put her arms around her and give her a hug. But now Mum was at the bottom of the stairs, shouting, "Come on I need some help here."

And by the time they'd sorted out the plastic sacks of things from their old life, it was too late to say or do anything.

Manuscript 3

Every day and night after that, I wore the ring tied around my neck on its linen braid. And I waited for him to return. There were so many things I needed to ask him. Who was Sekhmet? How would the ring with its hieroglyphics protect me from her? What would happen if I were to wear it? And why did he need my help?

At first I was downcast when he did not come. I looked for him everywhere. But time ran on. I was kept busy in my father's shop. It was only in the dead of night that his words came back to haunt my dreams.

Then one day early in March, I read in the Gazette *that an Egyptian mummy 'with all its hieroglyphics' was on show at the Head and Combe Inn on the Strand. Surely, I thought, this must be fate at work, and I its beneficiary.*

Telling my mother that I had an errand to do for my father, I put on my cloak and patten overshoes and slipped out of the house. I was determined to go and see the mummy at once, for I prayed the hieroglyphics would unlock the secret of my ring.

༄༅ ༄༅

It was while I was on my way to the Head and Combe that I saw him again. He was standing at the corner of Butcher Row and the Strand. A mass of people, carts and horses swirling about him in the foul and smoky air, as if he was at the quiet centre of a great storm.

I stood stock-still, my hand clutching at the ring, and I thought he looked straight at me. I felt faint, and for a moment closed my eyes. When I opened them again he was gone and the space where he had been was filled with people.

༄༅ ༄༅

When I arrived at last at the inn, the rope-walker I had seen at the fair was there before me, entertaining the crowd. And so great was the number of people come to see the mummy, I thought I should never get inside. But I pushed and squeezed, trod on toes and elbowed my way through the great press of people until, trembling with excitement, I had my first glimpse of it.

I had never seen one before, though I had read in the Histories *of Herodotus how the Egyptians turned their dead into mummies. How the embalmers pulled out the brain through the nostrils with an iron hook. How the flank of the corpse was laid open with a flint knife and the contents of the stomach removed. Then the cavity was rinsed out with palm wine, filled with aromatics, sewn up and placed in natron. When 70 days had passed, the body was washed and wrapped from head to toe in strips of linen, smeared with gum.*

Just as we swaddle babies as soon as they are born, I thought, so the Egyptians swaddled their dead for the journey and re-birth into the afterlife.

The mummy rested in a gilded wooden coffin. The lid of the coffin, fashioned in the form of a young woman, lay to one side. Her image took my breath clean away. The fullness of her lips. The straightness of her nose. Her black-rimmed eyes soft as a doe's. Her arms were folded across her breast. Heavy ropes of black hair lay on her shoulders. Her tunic was painted to look like folded linen and was covered in hieroglyphics.

I was close enough now to reach out a hand and touch her. Close enough to look inside the coffin. I was not afraid of what I might see. I had been at my grandmother's bedside when she died of the ague. I had seen thieves and murderers, men and women both, hung high from the gibbets on Tower Hill and at Tyburn. I had seen the rotting bodies of traitors picked clean by the kites and the crows. I had even seen an embalmed body. That of Sir Thomas Viner. He had died in the May of last year, but had not been buried until the June. My father told me how embalming fluids stopped his body putrefying in the summer heat. But I had never seen a body such as this; kept from decay for so very many years.

Someone had started to unwind the linen bands from around her. Her cheeks and eyes were sunken. Her skin, stained brown as amber, was stretched tight over the bones of her skull, and what little hair she had left was a dull red. I saw that the ring finger of her right hand was missing.

She must once have been beautiful, but was so no longer, and I felt a surge of pity for her. I should not like to be poked and gawped at by strangers when I die, I thought. If only I could read the hieroglyphics, I might know her name at least.

"It is Nefertaru. I found her in Egypt and brought her safe home with me." The Doctor was standing close beside me, and now the room was deathly quiet and the door shut firm. The great press of people had melted away like mist over the river at sunrise.

His hand guided mine to a group of hieroglyphics. "Her name and age at death are written here. She was just 14 years old and was a priestess and dancer at the Temple of Sekhmet."

"And," I asked, hardly able to breathe, feeling the heat of his hand on mine, "do the other hieroglyphics tell her story?"

"They are spells said to protect the soul as it travels from this world into the next. But they must be written and spoken faultlessly, or the spells will be flawed and the soul will be lost for ever. See here," he pointed to a hieroglyphic. "Someone has been careless... or wicked. They have written NefARtaru and not NefERtaru."

He laughed, as if the thought of a soul damned for ever gave him some pleasure.

I shivered. "How is it that you know these things? My father says there is no man alive who can read Egyptian writing."

"Your father is wrong... for I have mastered the skill of reading hieroglyphics." His gaze held me, as the poacher's lamp holds the rabbit, transfixed in its light. "But you must tell no one, for my life depends upon it. There are men prepared to kill for the knowledge I now possess."

And I believed him.

Chapter 4

It was nearly teatime and Claire was in the kitchen. Her mum was at the sink peeling potatoes. Any minute now she was going to ask about the envelope. Ask what was inside it. Oh well, Claire thought, she couldn't keep the ring hidden for ever. She'd have to show her mum sometime. Better get it over and done with.

"You know that envelope Grandma left for me?"

"Oh yes, the one stuffed with old bits of paper. I put it in the dresser drawer, Okay? Anything else in it? Lots of money I hope! We could do with some now."

"Just a ring. Look." She held out her hand. Her mum peered at it closely.

"Mmm. That's strange. It doesn't look like Grandma's sort of thing at all. I don't ever remember seeing her wear it. Do you?"

Claire shook her head.

"It looks Egyptian doesn't it? Go on, take it off and let's see what it looks like on me." Her mum was holding out her hand.

"I can't." Claire was pulling at it, but the more she pulled, the tighter it seemed to grip her finger. And anyway she knew it wouldn't fit her mum. She had big hands, just like Grandma's.

"Soap will do it."

But it didn't, and Claire breathed a sigh of relief when the six o'clock news came on the radio. Someone had dropped dead on the underground; the Central line at St. Paul's station. A new strain of bird flu. The seventh victim in the last six weeks and now doctors were predicting an epidemic. A modern day Great Plague.

Claire's mum stopped peeling and let the potato fall back into the bowl. "Well, well, wouldn't Grandma have been pleased to hear that? A plague… and on her doorstep too. You know she was always hoping that would happen. So she could study it at first hand."

"But that was her job, Mum, wasn't it? Of course she would have been interested in it."

Grandma was a professor who'd lectured all over the world on the spread of epidemic diseases.

Who had a special interest in the history and cause and spread of bubonic plague. Who'd written books about it.

"Not a job, Claire. Not just an ordinary, everyday job. What Grandma did was a vocation."

Claire had noticed how her mum's face always looked pinched and sour when she talked about Grandma's work. It looked like that now.

"Didn't she ever tell you how on her fourteenth birthday she was given some sodding sheaf of papers, by *her* grandmother, who said it was a manuscript written at the time of the Great Plague? And how, from that day on, she'd been hooked."

Manuscript, thought Claire. Was it the same sheaf of yellowing papers Grandma had left her?

"Do you know what happened to it?" Claire asked.

"Don't know. Don't care," snapped her mum. "It's just a shame she didn't put as much energy into looking after her only child as she did into researching plagues. *and* all that other rubbish she was so obsessed with."

She seemed so angry about it that when she picked up the potato and started peeling it again, the knife slipped and sliced into her finger.

Blood seeped into the flesh of the potato, staining it red. "Even now, just look what she's made me do!"

* * *

Claire's mum didn't mention the ring again for days. There were just too many other things for her to worry about. Grandma's will for one. Her mum thought she would inherit everything. Who else was there? But she couldn't be quite sure, because they hadn't ever really got on. And maybe everything would be left to Claire and Micky, in trust.

"From the minute I was born…" Claire's mum, talking while she looked in the hall mirror. Checking her make-up before she went out to see the solicitor. Making a face at her reflection so the words came out all distorted. "I was such a disappointment."

Claire was sitting on the stairs, hunched up, elbows on knees, face cupped in her hands, watching. Taking in every last little thing her mum did. The way she put on her lipstick. Smoothed out her eyebrows. Checked for stray hairs and new wrinkles. Centred the crystal she wore for luck on the gold chain around her neck.

"She always wanted a daughter with red hair." Claire's mum frowned. Her hand went up to touch her hair. It had once been an ordinary brown, just like Micky's. Now it was carefully coloured a beautiful glossy chestnut. She gave it a little satisfied pat. "That's the only thing she'd tell me about my father. He had red hair. Red-gold hair. It was like she thought it was the most important thing about him. As if she'd wanted him just for that!"

She turned and looked straight at Claire. "Of course when you were born, she was over the moon. I'd never seen her so excited. 'At last,' she said, as if I'd finally done something right. That really made me cross. It didn't make her love me any more – but she loved you."

Did she? Claire would never have guessed. Not in a million years. Grandma had always been so fierce and strict and unbending. "You need to be strong to survive in this world. Strong and independent-minded," she'd said. "Never let your heart rule your head, or destruction will follow."

So when her friend Katrin had said she was going off to meet up with some boy she'd met on the Internet, Grandma's words had popped into her head and she'd found herself telling

Katrin that it was a dangerous thing to do.

"You could get murdered like that girl on the news last week. I can't let you go. I have to tell."

"And if you do," Katrin had said, "I won't be your friend any more."

* * *

"But I had to stop her, didn't I?" Claire desperately wanted someone to tell her she'd done the right thing. "I was scared she might have ended up dead if I didn't. And now she's not speaking to me."

They had been at Grandma's house: Claire, Micky and her mum and dad, sitting round the big mahogany table, having Sunday lunch.

Grandma had reached across the table, clutched Claire's hand fiercely and said, "You must always do what is right, Claire. Remember that, even if what happens after is frightening and dangerous."

She'd wanted to snatch her hand away, because her Grandma's behaviour was making her feel really uncomfortable. "Oh, Grandma," she'd said, "Katrin not being my friend isn't that scary!"

"No. But what is going to happen will be and

you will need all the help I can give you. I should never have left it so late…"

* * *

Now Grandma was dead. Myocardial infarction. Heart attack. Claire's mum had found her, sitting bolt upright in bed. A cup of tea gone cold beside her on the chest of drawers. Eyes wide open still, in surprise and shock and her hand on the newspaper with its headline:

'BIRD FLU SWEEPS HONG KONG'

She'd been dead for two days.

* * *

"Right, I'm off." Claire's mum was already halfway out of the front door. "Look after Micky. Don't let her eat all the biscuits. I'll be back about lunchtime." Then she slammed the door so hard, the stained-glass panels in it rattled.

Claire sat still on the stairs for a moment. Listened for the sound of the car starting and pulling away, then jumped up and went to look for Micky.

She was in the back room, next to the kitchen. Where the TV was. And the DVD player. And the Xbox, now that they'd brought it over from the old house.

"Do you want to watch a film?" Claire asked. "I could make some popcorn and we could watch one together." But Micky was busy. Playing some complicated game of her own. So absorbed she didn't even answer.

For a minute, Claire just looked at her. Then she sighed loudly. "I'll be around. Shout if you want me." But she wouldn't. Not for ages. Not until she was hungry.

So Claire went out and stood in the hall, wondering what on earth she could do. The whole summer stretching ahead, hot and empty. Whatever had happened between her mum and dad, it looked as if she and Mum and Micky would be living in Grandma's house from now on. In a whole different, unfamiliar part of London. She didn't know a single person here, except Micky and her mum.

If she was back at home, her *real* home, she'd be out all the time, hanging around with friends. Now she was stuck in and having to look after

Micky, because her mum was out all the time instead. Oh God. She could feel the terrible dead weight of boredom pressing down on her already and the holidays had only just started. A whole six weeks stuck in this house, with nowhere to go and no one to see. And no holiday either this year, unless they went with Dad to Cornwall, to see his sister Annie and her children. Jessica who was Micky's age and little Jo who was still a baby. What was she going to do? How would she get through it? How would she get through the *next few hours*?

* * *

At first it was exciting going from room to room, peering into drawers and cupboards. Riffling through everything Grandma had kept so neat and ordered. Thinking, *She'd have gone mental if she'd caught me doing this*. Especially poking around in her study. She looked idly around at the shelves of books; mostly about epidemics and disease, but some about the history of the circus, jugglers, tightrope walkers... another of Grandma's obsessions. Mmm. In one of those tall bendy clip things on the desk, there were two tickets...

she peered closer… for La Cirque du Sekhmet, in the Jubilee Gardens on the Embankment. The tickets were for a Wednesday, two days before her birthday. A birthday present? No. Grandma knew she hated circuses. Tucked underneath the tickets was a flyer advertising a stunt by the circus wire-walkers. A high-wire crossing of the Thames finishing in Jubilee Gardens on the Embankment. The date of the stunt, a week after her birthday, circled in Grandma's black felt-tip pen. Then she'd glanced at the papers on the desk. Notes for a lecture Grandma had been asked to give in Austria later that summer – 'The Great Plague of Vienna, 1679–1680'. In the margin and written in red ink, a word that made Claire stop for a moment and read on.

> *ABRACADABRA. Often used as a magic charm, sometimes written on a triangle of paper and worn tied about the neck on a red linen braid. It was said to guard against evil and sickness…*

She shivered, even though the room was hot and stuffy. The ring was making her finger throb. It was so tight she couldn't even twist it round.

I wish I'd never put it on, she thought, then, suddenly, she felt quite sure that Grandma had meant her to; was still trying to influence what she did, even after death.

Well, Claire wasn't having any of that. So she ran up to the bathroom. Soaped furiously around the ring and her finger again. But however hard she twisted, it still wouldn't come off.

Oil. Bath oil. That might do it… but it didn't and now there was a dark stain all down the front of her sweatshirt. She could feel hysteria rising up inside her. She picked her mum's nail file off the windowledge and stupidly thought she could saw the ring off. The file slipped in the oil and made a gouge in her finger and now it was bleeding. She got blood on her sweatshirt too.

Then she just pulled and pulled and pulled, until it seemed like all the colour had drained out of everything and she felt cold and clammy. She sat down quickly on the toilet seat. Called out, "Micky!" But the back-room door was shut and she couldn't or wouldn't hear. "MICKY!"

Now she had the same weird feeling that she'd had in Grandma's bedroom, of pressure, panic and fear. There was that smell again, musty and sweet. The same compelling feeling someone was calling her name. Pressing in close behind her and whispering in her ear. She needed to get out. Go downstairs to Micky. But she was afraid if she stood up she would faint. So she crawled on hands and knees out of the bathroom and along the landing. Shuffled on her bottom, bump, bump, bump, down the stairs. Had just reached the last step when the back-room door opened.

"Micky!"

Micky came out, trailing a buzz of noise, singing tunelessly, but loudly, along with music only she could properly hear, and went into the kitchen.

Claire took a deep breath and stood up. Her legs felt wobbly, but her head felt clearer. She followed Micky, who was standing over an open dresser drawer, pulling things out, sifting around, looking for something. Claire clutched at her shoulder, making her jump. She looked startled and then pulled out the earpiece, spilling music as she did. "What?"

Claire had been going to say she'd felt really ill and needed Micky to help her, but…

"Nothing. What are you doing?"

"Looking for my Star Mix. I had a whole bag

and now it's gone. Mum's always tidying things away. I thought she might have put them in here."

"They're in the next drawer along. I saw her do it."

"Oh thanks!" said Micky and in a flash she had the sweets and was gone again. Leaving the first drawer open and empty.

Claire sighed. She started to put all the rubbish heaped on the table back in the drawer. And there, right at the bottom of the pile, was Grandma's envelope. She reached in and pulled out the sheaf of yellowing, brittle papers, tied with a red linen braid that still had the remains of a wax seal stuck to it.

She pulled out a chair and sat down. Slipped off the red braid. Held the two pieces of the seal together. Saw that the imprint in the wax matched the carving on her ring exactly. Another piece in the puzzle. Then she counted the pages out. Tried to read the first one. But the writing was cramped and spiky-looking and the writer had made use of every spare centimetre. Lines criss-crossed from left to right and from top to bottom. And there were splatters of black ink, making it almost illegible. But on the first page there was a name, Mary, Martha... no... Margrat? A surname beginning with a J? And on the second page, a date. The 27th day of February 1665.

She knew that date. The year the Great Plague had swept across London killing thousands. She shivered. Let the page fall from her hand. Plague. Black Death. Sickness. Fever. Imagine if those scratchy-looking words were written by someone just about to die of it.

Trying not to breath in, she shuffled the papers hurriedly together and, putting them back in the envelope, she leaned across and dropped it into the dresser drawer. She slammed the drawer shut, not noticing that her arm had swept the braid onto the floor. Then she hurriedly got up and went across to the sink, where she scrubbed and scrubbed her hands with soap. She turned on the hot tap and held her hands under the water until they turned pink with the heat.

"What are you doing?" Micky had come back into the kitchen and was standing right behind her.

"What does it look like, you idiot? And don't creep up on me like that again. You frightened me to death." She felt really odd. Panicky. Like she was in the middle of a bad dream; knew she was, but still couldn't wake up.

"If I HAD frightened you to death" – Micky had that smug look she always got when she thought she was being clever – "you'd be dead and lying on the floor and..."

"Shut up and get out of my way."

She flicked water in Micky's face. She pushed her hard and Micky pushed her back. Then as she tried to get past her, Micky put out a foot to trip her up.

"Nice try," Claire said, jumping over it and reaching back to make a grab for Micky and pull her down.

"Ginger nut. Ginger nut." Micky ducked out of the way and pushed past her out into the hall.

Claire had just caught up with her, was holding onto her right arm while Micky was squirming and thrashing about, when the doorbell went.

They stopped fighting and looked at one another for a moment. Then Micky pulled away and ran off. Bang! The back-room door slammed.

Shouting, "I'll get you later, you little stinker... just you wait." Claire went to the front door and, slipping on the safety chain, opened the door just wide enough to peek out.

There was a man on the step, turned away

from her, looking back down the street. He was tall and had thick dark hair just curling onto the shoulders of his black jacket. And he was leaning on a black lacquered walking stick.

"Yes?"

He turned and Claire looked up into eyes that weren't like any she had ever seen before. Such a deep, dark brown, they were almost black.

She stood, not moving a muscle, quite mesmerised by him. She had the feeling that, though she had never met him before in her life, she somehow knew him and he knew her.

She tensed herself, ready to slam the door if he tried to step closer. Felt the ring, hot and tight on her finger.

But he stood quite still, his eyes unblinking, focused on hers.

"Yes?" She was starting to feel anxious now and impatient. Who was he and what did he want? Was he trying to sell something? Claire didn't think so. He looked too expensively dressed. He was wearing a very finely woven linen shirt under a long black jacket. He had beautifully cut, narrow-legged black trousers and dark, blood red, soft leather shoes fastened with a buckle. He had a black leather bag slung across his shoulder.

But he looked tired. There were lines and deep shadows around his eyes. Hungry eyes. "I…" He was staring at her with such an intensity that she was starting to feel spooked. "I was hoping to speak to Jill Cottrell. Are you…?"

His voice was deep but soft. She had to lean in towards him to catch what he was saying. And there was something odd about the way he spoke. What was it? Was he foreign? Maybe. She wasn't sure.

"Jill? No that's my mum." And she was about to say that her mum was out, but stopped herself in time. Better not to tell him there were no adults in the house. "She's in the shower. She'll be ages yet."

"Ah. I see. Perhaps you could give her this?"

He held out a card. Small and white, with a gold edge.

As she took it, something scratched her hand. It was then that she noticed not only the perfectly manicured nails, but the ring he wore. A diamond set in sharp claws of gold. On the third finger of his right hand. And there was something else. She couldn't quite work it out, but he smelled of something familiar. What was it? Her eyes widened

in shock and she shut the door on him quickly,
feeling her heart miss a beat.

Oh yes, she recognised it now. The same smell
as in Grandma's bedroom. So sweet and seductive.
As if there was an apple-and-cinnamon pie baking
in a kitchen full of scented summer flowers.

She could see him through the glass, still
standing there. Then, thank God, he turned and
walked away.

She looked at the card.

> Robert Benoit
> Dealer in Antiquities
> Darke House
> Ivybridge Lane
> The Strand
> London

Then a phone number.

Benoit. A foreign name? That would explain
the way he talked and dressed.

She put the card down on the hall table, next
to the phone and a magazine open at the small ads
and one circled in red pen.

Then she forgot about it because, not long

after, her mum came in and couldn't wait to tell her the good news.

"She did leave everything to me. Everything! That is such a relief. Now we can stay here. And I know that I ought to wait for everything to be sorted legally, but I'm going to start having a clear-out right now!"

Claire didn't think it was a relief at all. She didn't like the house and all of Grandma's things that filled it up. It was dark and gloomy, and made her feel dark and gloomy too. Pictures covered every square inch of wall; mostly old maps of London. And there were shelves and shelves of books. But even so, it seemed heartless when Grandma had only been dead for a few weeks.

"You can't do that," she said. "Sell off Grandma's whole life just like that."

"I'm not going to sell it off. Well not until I've got everything checked first. There might be some valuable things. Like that Egyptian green box thingy in Grandma's bedroom. That might be worth something."

She was trying to sound as if the thought had just popped into her head. Claire wasn't fooled. She guessed that her mum had had her eye on it for ages. Maybe even before Grandma had died. Well she wasn't going to have it.

"That's mine." Claire sounded determined. She was.

"And what makes you think that?" Claire's mum's voice sounded clipped and controlled. A red flush was spreading up her neck. Always a bad sign. It meant she was getting angry.

Because, Claire thought, *the ring is somehow the key to unlocking the box.*

But if she said that, she'd have to show that it was. And she couldn't. *Because it isn't time yet.* A voice, whispering inside her head, but coming from somewhere else. Claire looked around, startled.

"Claire! Are you listening to me?" Her mum was getting impatient, tapping a finger irritably on the edge of the table. Her eyes had narrowed.

"Yes!"

"Mmm. Well, I've already contacted someone about it. A specialist. I've asked him to come and take a look at it and whatever else there is in the house. If there's anything valuable, I'm selling."

Claire thought now about the man who had come to the door. About the card he had given her and the magazine on the hall table, with the ad circled in red pen. "What does he look like, this specialist?"

"What? How should I know? I just left a message on his answerphone. Now I'm going to make a start clearing out. Want to help?"

But Claire didn't. The minute her mum was out of the way, she went back and looked at the ad.

Collector seeks early Egyptian artefacts, similar to the one in the illustration below.

She looked at the coloured illustration. She could see why her mum had called the number. It showed a box that looked remarkably like Claire's emerald-green casket.

Then she picked up the card, re-read and quickly pocketed it. Maybe he wouldn't call again, she thought, knowing deep down that he would.

* * *

Teatime and they were all squeezed around the little kitchen table. Eating sausage, mash and baked beans.

They had to eat together now. Claire's mum insisted on it. No more slouching in front of the television. No more taking food up to their bedrooms. No more doing things the way they had in their old life. There was going to be a fresh start. Everything was going to be better from now on.

"Isn't this nice?"

Claire looked at her mum. Her mouth was smiling, but her eyes weren't. And she couldn't really be happy, could she? Because how could moving out of your old house and leaving your husband make you happy?

"The mash is a bit lumpy," said Micky. She was pushing it around her plate with her fork. "But it's Okay."

"I'm not hungry." Claire looked down at her plate. At the sausages glistening with fat. At the sticky, grainy, grey pile of potato. The scratch on her hand was starting to hurt really badly. It looked angry and red. And the ring was so tight on her finger now it was making it throb.

Micky looked up. "Wow! You've gone a funny colour. You've gone green. I've never seen anyone go green before. Mum, Claire's green!"

Claire's head was filling up with noise, like

a great roaring wind. She felt as if she was
burning. Now she was floating; drifting up and
away like ash from a fire. Someone was shouting,
but from a long way away. What were they saying?
She struggled to make out the words.

"Put your head down between your knees.
Now!" Claire could feel her mum's hand pressing
down on the back of her head. "Micky, get a
bucket."

But it was too late. Claire's jeans were covered
in vomit and she started to cry.

* * *

Now she was lying in Grandma's bed, curled up on
her side, afraid to move in case she was
sick again, but wishing she was in her own room.
Because, even with her eyes closed and turned away
from it, she could sense that the box was there, on
the chair by the bed. And the smell. That curious
sweet smell. It was still there, faint but insistent.

"You'll be okay for a minute, won't you?" her
mum was saying. "You don't mind being in
Grandma's bed do you? Only you can't share with
Micky. Not if you're being sick."

Her mum didn't wait for her to answer. She just snatched up Claire's clothes, dropped in a heap by the bed, and left.

Now Claire was alone, fear flooded in and washed over her. She felt really poorly and she just couldn't think straight.

I wish Dad was here, she thought. He'd be happy just to sit by the bed and he would understand why she was feeling really scared. Couldn't stop thinking about the yellowing sheaf of papers and panicking stupidly.

"Look," he'd say, "of course you haven't got the plague. You couldn't catch it after all this time. Not from just touching paper!"

But you could, Claire thought. She was sure that she'd read that you could.

"No," Dad would say, "It's just a virus. You'll get better. Everything will go back to normal, you'll see."

But he wasn't there and she missed him so much. And she didn't feel better. She felt much worse. Any tiny movement and giant waves of nausea broke over her. She clung to the side of the bed now, like a drowning man desperate to stay afloat. With her eyes closed, pictures flickered across the inside of her eyelids, like a rolling film. Faces she didn't recognise peered in at her; voices blurred and distorted, as if the words were spoken underwater. Images of a boy, in costume, dancing fast and furious high up on a wire. He was beckoning to her. Then he swung down and ran towards her. She could see his face. His eyes glittering. His lips moving, but no sound coming out. There was only a background roar and rattle. Like a train hurtling at breakneck speed through a long, dark tunnel. On and on until everything was dazzlingly bright and silent... except for the sound of her mum and dad bickering. Backwards and forwards. Backwards and forwards, just as if she wasn't there and couldn't hear what they were saying.

"My God, Jill, I can't believe you didn't call the doctor. Just look at her. Don't you ever listen to the news? There's been 60 cases of bird flu in London this last week. Supposing she had that? She could have been dead now. And please don't tell me you were giving her any of your crackpot herbal remedies?"

"Dad," Claire said, her voice coming out all faint and whispery. "It's okay. I'm all right.

And Mum hasn't given me anything, honestly."
Claire reached out to touch her dad's arm, but her
mum snatched at Clare's hand, pulling it to her
and squeezing it tight, saying, "And she isn't dead.
And I'm not stupid. It was a 24-hour gastric bug;
that's all. It's been going round. She's fine now.
She'll be up and jumping around in no time.
You're making too much fuss. Kids get sick all the
time. And don't you dare lecture me about taking
care of my children. Not now."

Why does she have to be so horrid? thought Claire.
I mean, she left him, didn't she?

Manuscript 4

Now I see that as I looked down at Nefertaru's mummy the Doctor bound me to him as he told me his secret, how he had come to find the spells and decipher them. For he said that men would willingly murder for such knowledge. That if anyone knew he had the spells and could decipher them, then his life would be in great danger. And I felt proud that a man such as Nicholas Robert Benedict would place his trust in the hands of a girl, not yet 14 years old. So I promised. I swore on my mother and father's lives that no living soul would drag his secret from me. He said he was sure that I'd heard talk in my father's shop of a lost book, The Hermetica.

I had, for much had been made of it. How it contained the magical secrets of Thoth, Egyptian god of all knowledge. How any man finding it would be privy to those secrets and become supremely powerful. How he would be immortal and have control over all things in

Nature. Every single plant or creature that lives on the Earth. A power not known to any human creature since Adam and Eve were banished from the Garden of Eden. But my father had called it skimble-skamble stuff, saying that if there was really such a book in existence, then surely someone would have found it. And having found it, would have used its power for good or ill.

"That is true, Margrat," said the Doctor. "If any man could be master of the universe, would he not be tempted?"

"No!" I said, distressed at his words. "For only God is master of the universe and all things in it."

His face darkened, as if a cloud had scuttered across the moon. "What comfort is there in that, for the many who will soon die a cruel death from the plague? Do you truly believe that all those who suffer deserve it? Even babies, just as I was, innocent of wickedness, left all alone and crying piteously and uncared for, while their mothers and fathers lie dead beside them?"

I could see that he was in the grip of some powerful emotion and watching his face contort with the pain of it left me shaken. But I answered as I had been taught. That it was not for us to know the ways of God. That there was a reason for everything. That it was blasphemy to question His will.

He smiled. But it was a cold, dark smile. "Then it must have been God's will that when travelling through the desert near Alexandria, I stumbled upon a stone tablet, carved with a text in three scripts: Greek, demotic and hieroglyphic. I was able to read the Greek and demotic scripts and I could see that they were both the same list, written by Egyptian priests, of all the good things the pharaoh had done for the people of Egypt."

"Was the text written in hieroglyphics the same list too? For if it was, then you might read it!" A spark of excitement was kindled in my breast at the thought of it.

"How clever of you to see that, Margrat. But I needed to study it to be sure. Back at my lodgings in Alexandria, I set to work translating the hieroglyphics. It was to be a long time before I could manage even a little. But at last I gained mastery over it."

My hand flew up to my mouth.

His eyes held mine. "And all the while I continued my other work; searching out the tombs of the Egyptian kings. Uncovering their treasures and sending them back to England to be put on show or sold. But then…" He took hold of my hand and, turning it palm up, kissed it.

For a moment I forgot all about the stone tablet and thought only how the touch of his lips made me feel.

A powerful and exciting emotion I had never felt before.

"*On the last day of November,*" *he continued,*
"*I found, buried under the floor in Nefertaru's tomb,
a clay jar packed full of scrolls, each covered in
hieroglyphics.*"

Nefertaru! The very mummy on show before us now.

"*I took the scrolls back to my lodgings and began
work at once on their translation. Each scroll contained
one part of what I soon came to believe, was* The
Hermetica. *As I was able to read each spell, I grew
more full of life and energy. I hardly needed to sleep.
My aches and pains disappeared. My hair grew thick
and dark again. My skin became unlined and smooth.
And I have not yet unlocked the secrets of the 21st spell,
which I believe to be the most powerful spell of all. The
one, I hope, that will allow me to raise the dead. The
spell that will not simply keep me youthful... but will
make me immortal! Able to live for ever, as God does.*"
*His hand squeezed mine so tightly that I cried out and
tried to pull free of him. But he was too strong.*

I looked at him then in shock and awe. A man
*desiring to be God. The breathtaking arrogance of it
made me tremble with fear and excitement.*

"*But whoever had placed the scrolls in the tomb
had put a curse on them. For as I worked on the scrolls,*

Sekhmet, the Egyptian goddess of pestilence, sent her plague-bearing messengers to find me. All around me, people began to fall ill and I fled from Egypt, carrying the scrolls in my leather bag. But the carriage I took from Chatham to London was set upon by thieves and the bag was taken. Now I did not have the scrolls, I was in mortal fear for my life."

A leather bag and full of scrolls! But what of the ring?

"Then all is lost, sir," I said, feeling a curious mixture of fear that I would be found out and excitement at the thought of it.

"I feared that too, Margrat. When the scrolls were stolen from me and I could not recite them every day, I was afraid that I would die. I began to feel deathly tired. My face in the mirror looked sallow and lined. My hair began to streak with grey. But I knew the scrolls were somewhere in London. For the messengers of Sekhmet were still following the scrolls, bringing plague on their heels like a pack of unruly and savage dogs. When the plague reached London, I knew the scrolls must be nearby."

"Plague is nothing new," I said quickly. "People have died of it and always will."

"But this time it is different, Margrat. Mark my

words carefully. It has begun. The plague is already here and will become more virulent. Many will die, as they did in Alexandria. I cannot save them yet."

"You may die, too," I said, dread and hope both rising in me at the thought of it. For though his words made me very afraid, unaccountably I still longed to be with him, stand close, breathe in his sweet smell and hear his voice.

"Yes. I was mortally afraid," he said. "So I went to every bookseller and dealer in the City... finding nothing until I came to your father's shop."

I knew my skin was flushed a deep red.

"Your father said I was in luck. A number of scrolls had come into his possession, just that very morning. He showed them to me. And they were my scrolls, still in my leather bag and so I bought them from him."

"And now that you have them, you may translate them all," I said hurriedly, for his eyes were still fixed upon me.

"Do not rejoice yet, Margrat. Remember, there is one spell, the 21st, that is still locked away where I cannot reach it. But I have the key now and I mean to use it." He stroked my hair and let his hand fall to my neck and to the ring. The ring had been with the scrolls, but still he said nothing about that. I could

not hold my tongue any longer. He must know now that I had stolen it.

"And what of my ring?"

His face, for a fleeting moment, had the look of a lost soul shown a glimpse of Paradise. Then he said, "Ah yes, the ring is a powerful charm that will protect you from the plague. I confess: I took it from Nefertaru's mummy... just as you surely took it out of my leather bag."

I raised my hands as if to untie the braid and give him back the ring, but he stopped me, saying, "No, you were meant to have it. I see that now."

But I could not help looking down at Nefertaru's right hand. I shivered and he saw that I did.

"Come, Margrat, she no longer has need of it. Be grateful I took it and you now have it and are protected from the plague. For until I have the 21st spell, I will not be able to raise the dead and lead them into Paradise. Create Heaven here on Earth, as I believe it was always meant to be. But once that power is mine, I will do it. And would that not be a wonderful thing?"

The Doctor took my hand and led me out into the street. "Look around you, Margrat. Look carefully. What do you truly see?"

To my horror, the hustle and bustle, energy and high spirits of London seemed nothing now but filth and smoke and noise. It was as if I had tumbled straight into the bowels of Hell.

"There, do not be afraid." The Doctor turned me to him, enfolded me in his cloak and held me close. "You are safe with me. You will be always."

His voice, soft as swansdown, heady and seductive as frankincense, mesmerising as the high, pure sound of a boy's voice singing at Vespers. "Tell me, Margrat." His voice ever more seductive. "Where is your God in all this? I tell you, if he exists, then he has abandoned his creation to the Devil... and all his priests."

Pressed in so close to him, I could hear his heart beat clear and sure and strong. Doubt crept into my soul silently, like a rat hiding in a cellar waiting till all is quiet and dark to move up into the body of the house and gnaw through its very fabric.

I ran from it and from him, as fast as the rat runs from the dog. But I knew I could not outrun it, or him.

സൗള്ള

When I arrived home I had quite forgotten that I had lied to my mother. Told her I had an errand to do for my father, so that I might go to see the mummy,

Nefertaru at the Head and Combe Inn. But my mother had not forgotten. She demanded to know at once where I had been, for it seemed, she said, that my father knew nothing of any errand! Her temper was so foul she did not at first notice my distress.

"I... have... been," I said, struggling to catch my breath, "to see the mummy on show... at the Head and Combe."

"You bone-headed, idle..." She raised her hand to slap me.

"Where I met... with the Doctor."

On the instant, my mother's hand dropped and her face was all smiles. "Why did you not say that at once?"

He has power over people, I thought, even without his spells. Money. Connections to all the most important people in the land. A fine, upright figure and a handsome face. An unshakable conviction that he is right in everything he thinks and does.

"Such an honest, godly man," she said and I longed to wipe the smile clear from her face by telling her of his blasphemies. But I had promised not to. Besides, she would not believe me. Worse still, she would rage at my father; say that too much learning had addled my brain.

"*I have heard that he is well known at Court and has a fine house, newly built behind the Strand... and lives quite alone there.*"

I refused to look at her, for I knew what she was thinking and was ashamed. For even now, when I had heard him question the very existence of God and knew his intentions, I was powerfully drawn to him.

"*I will send a note to him directly and ask him to come to dinner tomorrow.*" *Her temper had cooled and she sounded mighty pleased with herself for having thought of it.* "*Go and tidy yourself and then come down to the kitchen. We must start preparations at once for tomorrow's meal.*"

∞℮ ℮∞

I went to bed that night deathly tired, but when I blew out the candle, sleep would not come. Instead I lay there in the dark thinking of the 20 scrolls. How I had held them in my hands and not known the power of them. But where was the 21st spell the Doctor had spoken of? Not a scroll then... for he spoke of a key and seemed sure he would unlock the spell soon. And what of my ring? Though the Doctor said it was just a powerful charm against plague and nothing more, I began to doubt him. *For I have seen in my father's shop how men behave when they covet a rare and valuable book. They pretend they have no real interest in it. Their eyes look away into the distance. They run their fingers across its cover as if it is nothing, but their breathing quickens and when they ask the price, their voice betrays their excitement.*

Unbidden, excitement welled up inside me too and when at last I did fall asleep. I dreamed that I was in an immense shadowy hall. Before me, a man who had the head and long pointed snout of a black dog stood next to a pair of golden scales. I looked on as my heart, still beating, was weighed against a feather and I said, "Oh heart, do not act as witness against me! I have not done what the gods hate. I have not known that which should not be known." But I lied. And so my heart, heavy with sin, tipped the balance and was thrown to a monster who, leaping out of the shadows, devoured it.

Chapter 5

Claire's mum had found the card when she'd washed her jeans.

"Why didn't you tell me he'd called?" she'd said, standing at the foot of Grandma's bed, looking cross and exasperated.

"I just forgot, that's all. Okay?"

"And what was he like? Did he seem nice?"

"How do I know? He was just a man that's all. Nothing special."

That wasn't true, but she wasn't going to tell her mum that. No, let her forget all about him and the box. But she wasn't about to. Oh no.

"Hand me that box. I'll keep it safe."

"It's *my* box." Claire said. But it was no good. Her mum was determined to have it. In seconds she had it in her arms and was marching out of the door with it.

Claire didn't have the energy to argue any more.

She still didn't feel well. Maybe her dad could sort it out next time he came round to the house. If her mum would let him in, that is. Still, she'd ring him later, when he was back from work. And she'd ask him to come.

She rolled onto her side and looked at the chair; at the empty space where the box had been. She was sure Grandma had wanted her to have the box. She would have to stop her mum selling it, but had no idea how. It was no good. She couldn't wait. She had to ring her dad.

She pushed back the covers, swung her legs over the side of the bed and tried to stand up. Her legs felt weak and wobbly.

Her backpack with her mobile in it was hanging where she'd left it, at the bottom of the stairs. Not far, but it took an enormous effort of will to fetch it. She managed though and made it back into bed without her mum hearing. She slumped on the pillows with a huge sigh of relief. Then she fished out her phone and called her old house number. But there was only the sound of her dad's voice on the answer phone.

Sorry. John is not available at the moment. Please leave your number and he'll get back to you.

And when she called his mobile, it was switched off.

* * *

Days passed. She was up and out of bed now. Feeling much better until she heard the doorbell or the phone ring. Then her stomach muscles clenched into a tight knot. Hoping it might be her dad calling. Afraid it might be that man. She was sure he'd be back. That her mum would have called him again. Asked him to ring when she thought Claire would be out. So Claire made sure she stayed put. Even though being in the house was making her stir crazy. She hadn't been out anywhere for days and days now. Even going to the circus seemed tempting. She had told Jade about Grandma's tickets and Jade had offered to go with her.

Claire had moved back into the room she shared with Micky again. But she still fell asleep every night thinking about the box and about him. Then she'd dream. Nightmares. And she'd wake, plucking at the ring on her finger and drenched in sweat.

She needed to get the box back. She looked

everywhere for it. Even waited until her mum was in the bath and then searched her bedroom. But she couldn't find it. Maybe her mum had taken the box to him? Maybe she'd sold it already?

* * *

He came when she wasn't expecting it. Catching her off guard.

Friday evening, she was out the front, putting rubbish in the bin. She was thinking how horrible everything smelled. The sharp, acrid smell of urine, petrol, exhaust fumes. There hadn't been any rain for weeks now. Everything looked tired; covered in a fine layer of dirt. Even the roses were wilting, drifts of petals scattered across the pavement outside the house. Speckling the tarmac like an improbable fall of snow.

She let the bin lid drop and had just turned to go into the house when there was a sudden noise. The creak and squeal of the gate opening. She looked back and there he was, still carrying the leather bag. Still wearing the same white linen shirt, the same black trousers and collarless jacket, even in this terrible heat. Other people wore black jackets and trousers and white shirts. But these were different. Like when bell-bottomed hipsters had come back into fashion and her mum had got her old ones out and had started to wear them again. It wasn't any good. It didn't look right. You knew the difference straight away.

And there was something else. She didn't know what. But it unsettled her. Made her wary and the hairs on the back of her neck prickle and stand up.

"Your mother asked me to call."

"Mum!" She stood firm in the doorway. She wasn't going to let him in unless she absolutely had to. But when her mum came hurrying down the hallway, she invited him in at once. He stepped past Claire now and though she tried hard not to breathe in, she could still smell cinnamon and flowers.

"Come through." Her mum was leading him into the kitchen. Claire saw her take a key from her pocket, unlock the dresser cupboard, take out something and put it on the kitchen table.

So that's where she'd put the box! It had been right under her nose the whole time. How stupidly obvious was that.

Claire moved in closer, watching him intently. She could see his knuckles, white with tension as he gripped his walking stick. He reached out with his free hand and pulled the box towards him across the table. He let his stick fall with a clatter to the floor. But he scarcely noticed. His whole attention was focused on the box.

"What do you think?" Claire's mum bent down to pick up the walking stick. And something else she'd spotted under the dresser. The red linen braid. Claire hadn't realised that she'd dropped it. Now Claire's mum was twisting it absently around her fingers. "The box. Is it Egyptian?" She was trying to sound casual, matter of fact, but there was an edge to her voice. "Only there doesn't seem to be any way of opening it. I can't see any hinges or a keyhole or anything."

He looked up. His eyes focused in on the red braid, twisting around her mum's fingers and widened in shock. Then, for a fleeting second, he closed his eyes and looked... happy? No. Not happy exactly. But relieved. As if he had been lost in a dark place and all at once saw a glimmer of light that would lead him out.

"Would you like a cup of tea?" Her mum dropped the braid onto the table and went to fill the kettle. "Or coffee if you'd rather."

He picked up the braid quickly and slipped it into his jacket pocket. Why had he done that?

And now he was smiling. "Tea, no milk or sugar. Thank you. An Egyptian casket, yes. And there is a way of opening it. But you must have the key."

"But there's no keyhole, so how can there be a key?" Claire's mum sounded amused as if he'd just said something absurd.

Claire held her breath. Instinctively covered her right hand with her left, so the ring wouldn't show. Prayed he hadn't seen it already.

"Oh not a key as you mean it," he said, "but something that is an exact mirror image of the lock." He tipped the box towards Claire's mum. His finger traced the oval of the cartouche and the hieroglyphics in it.

"Like what?" her mum asked, looking puzzled; putting a plate of biscuits down on the table then turning back to pour out the tea.

Thank God she hasn't worked out what he means… Claire felt a moment's relief and then Micky appeared in the doorway.

"Oooh, chocolate biscuits." But she hesitated, seeing a stranger sitting at the table.

Then he smiled at her. Held out the plate. She went to take a biscuit.

"Hello," he said. "I'm Robert. I've come to look at your grandmother's box. I was just explaining about the key. How it would be something that was the mirror image of this…"

Micky looked. Her face lit up. "Oh that's easy," she said.

All eyes were on her.

"I bet it's Claire's ring."

Claire had to show him the ring then. Micky had tried to grab her hand. She'd pushed her away. But it was no good anyway. Now that her mum knew, she wouldn't have a minute's peace until she did. So she held out her hand and he took it; lifting it up so he could have a closer look. Close enough that she could feel his breath whisper against her fingers.

"Oh yes. I think you might be right." He looked up. Held her gaze.

And there is no surprise in his eyes, she thought, *because when he first came to the house he gave me his card and I took it, and he must have seen the ring then.*

"And do you know?" He was looking at Micky now. "It is very old. Middle Kingdom Egyptian.

Almost certainly it was worn by a priest or priestess at Sekhmet's temple. Sekhmet… the most powerful and terrible goddess, bringer of plagues and diseases."

Sekhmet… the name of the circus! Maybe that's why Grandma had bought the tickets? Another piece of the puzzle, Claire was sure of it, and maybe soon now it would start to take shape.

"Wicked!" said Micky. "Do you know loads about mummies and curses and stuff?"

"Well," he said, "I did live in Egypt once and…" His voice had dropped to a whisper. "I believe some scrolls I found buried under the floor of an ancient tomb had a curse placed on them, because…"

Micky's eyes were round as saucers.

"Sadly, everywhere I go now, sickness follows… people die. Horribly."

For a second there was silence. Then he made a face. Drew a hand across his neck. Made a gurgling sound in his throat.

Claire's mum laughed. Relief. For a split-second Claire could tell she'd thought he was serious.

Micky still did. "But you're not dead!"

"Ah no," he said. "You see, the scrolls I uncovered

were spells, and if I'm careful to say them every day, just before dawn," – he paused for effect – "then I cannot die."

Micky was hooked. "Uh! What, not ever?"

Claire twisted the ring round and round her finger. Watched his face as it seemed to be registering real emotions. Then she leaned across him and quickly pulled the box to her and pressed her ring into the cartouche on its side. Her mum and Micky looked hopeful. Expectant.

But he doesn't, she thought. *Because...* and the same words popped into her head again: *it isn't time yet.*

Manuscript 5

I awoke and lay awhile with the curtains drawn around my bed, not knowing what time of the day or night it was. For a few brief moments I felt warm and peaceful, though there was noise from outside. The clatter of carriage wheels on cobbles. The crow of the cockerel. The squeal of a pig. Jane snoring softly. And someone was shouting for a link boy to light the way, so I knew the sun was not yet risen.

I snuggled down, pulling the covers over my head. The feathers in the mattress folded around me, as if I was buried under a blanket of deep, warm snow. All sound was muffled, except for the steady thud of my heart beating. If only I could stay here, safe, for ever. If only I hadn't taken the ring.

I could hear my mother was up and about. Doors slammed. Her voice was getting louder and louder, shouting, "Margrat! Jane! Wake up you slug-a-beds. There is work to do."

Now I remembered. The Doctor was invited for dinner and he had sent word that he would come. I had not doubted it for a moment.

Jane was sent out to the Stocks Market early to buy a rabbit for a fricassee. Oysters, salmon and a lobster too, for my mother hoped to impress. The eminent doctor, Nicholas Benedict, was to dine at her table!

But by nine o'clock, Jane had still not come home and my mother, grown frantic, sent me out, still wearing my apron, to look for her. "If you find her, send her home at once. Then you must go to Cheapside to buy some salads from the herb market. Be quick as you can, for the Doctor will be here before we know it."

ℙℙ

Truly, I meant to be, for my mother was like the Devil when crossed. But then, just as I came to the corner of Milk Street, I saw a noisy crowd had gathered. A rope-walker had set up his poles and rope. I watched as he clambered up and started his walk. Though I knew perfectly well that he did not, just for a heartbeat, it seemed that he trod the air.

The crowd gasped and fell silent in wonder as he became an acrobat and danced upon the rope. Then, turning one last somersault, he made a deep bow, saying, "Merci mes amis," and we all began to shout and clap and the spell was broken.

But just as the rope-walker made to swing down, a man ran up crying, "The plague is upon us. Three are dead in Southwark."

৵৹ঌ ঌ৹৵

I knew at once what would happen, for I had seen it all before. An Italian blamed for a fire in Leadenhall Street was beaten about the head with an iron bar until the blood made a great pool about his feet. A Dutch sailor accused of being a spy was lynched by the mob. Now a Frenchman, a rope-walker, was to be blamed and set upon for bringing the plague into London.

I was right, for a great wave of people swept in on the rope-walker. He was pushed to the ground and kicked about the head and body mercilessly. He cried out. A woman screamed, "Dirty Frenchman. Kill him!" But just as the tide always turns, the crowd grew tired of their sport. For the rope-walker would not fight back and lay, curled up like a hedge-pig.

One by one the people slipped away, the street fell empty and silent and I slowly came out from the shadows where I had been hiding. I crept up to look at the rope-walker's body, lying where it had been kicked into the gutter and as I got closer, I drew in my breath sharp. Not at the sight of the blood, of which there was much, but at the rope-walker's age. For he looked just a little older than me and I knew him. He was the rope-walker I had watched at the Frost Fair and outside the Head and Combe.

I reached out my hand and touched his shoulder gently. Then I brushed his hair, fine as red silk, out of his eyes which were swollen and closed tight shut. He made no move, but his lips parted and I heard a long drawing in of breath, like the wind off the river, stirring the willow leaves.

I knelt down beside him in the dirt, hoping the Doctor was right and the ring would keep me safe from the plague. I felt for it, turning it round and round on its braid, thinking of Sekhmet and praying also to God to keep me safe from harm. Then I took the corner of my apron, spat on it and began to wipe his face clean. I tried to be as gentle as I could. But he cried out and his hands came up to shield his face, causing me to sit back on my heels, transfixed. For on the third finger of his right hand he wore a ring. A gold ring, fashioned the same as mine and with the same blue stone and hieroglyphics. How had he come by it? How was it that he wore it openly on his finger and lived, when the

Doctor had told me that to wear it so would prove fatal.
Who was he?

༄ༀ ༀༀ

But I had no time now to think on it, for life was
returning to the street and the bells of nearby St Giles had
started to ring. Ten o'clock! I knew that I must hurry
home, but I did not know what to do with the rope-
walker. Perhaps I should have given him a few of my
pennies and left him there. The streets always swarmed
with vagabonds, gypsies and beggars. Men, women and
children often died, uncared for in the gutter. One more
would make no difference. If I had been more my
mother's child, I would have left him and kept my
money. But I knew my father would want me to help him
so I decided to take the rope-walker back home with me.

At first he would not come. Eyes still shut, he
pushed my hand away, saying, "Non. Laissez-moi."

And though his lip was cut and English not his
native tongue, I understood his words clearly.

A crowd of people had started to gather again.
I could hear muttering. "The French dog still lies in the
gutter," said one.

"Call the raker and have him taken away," said
another.

Then a loud, red-faced woman stepped up and said, "Let us cut off his head and ask the hangman to boil it with herbs so that we might eat it." And all about her roared with laughter.

"You must come," I whispered urgently, tugging at his hand. "Or you will be killed and I would be sorry for it." I reached for the ring on its braid. I had taken to using it as a charm against bad luck. I do not think the rope-walker saw me do it, for his eyes looked still shut tight. But a moment later, he opened them and looked straight at me. Though he was clearly in pain, he gripped my hand and struggled to his feet.

"Here," I said. "Lean on me and I will take you to my house. It is close by."

The crowd followed us as far as Bow Lane, then stopped by a baker's that I knew was owned by a Dutchman. What mischief they did there I do not know, but I confess I was grateful they no longer followed us. We reached home safe.

☙ ❧

Jane must have returned home in my absence, for she came to the door and stood there, hands on hips, insolently barring the way. "Go shoe the goose," she said gleefully. "You are in trouble and no mistake.

Wait till the mistress sees you come home with a beggar boy, instead of the herbs you were sent for. You'll get a thrashing."

I said nothing but, as I pushed past her, I contrived to tread hard on her foot with my patten.

Hearing the scream, my father stepped out into the hall. "What is the matter? Are there thieves at the door?"

"Not a thief, Father," I said, "but a poor boy who was set upon in the street and beaten. Should I have left him to die there?"

Before he could answer, my mother appeared, wiping her hands down her apron and looking flushed. "Boy? What boy is this? The Doctor will be here before we know it and the dinner will be only half cooked. I have no time to be looking after beggar boys."

While we argued, the rope-walker slid down in the doorway and turned deathly pale.

"See," screeched my mother. "He has brought the plague to our house. Now we will all die!"

"The only one likely to die is the boy!" I answered back. "And you will have killed him."

I thought it likely my mother might die herself... of an apoplexy. For her face, now so close to mine I could smell the sourness of her breath, was the colour of a boiled lobster. She took me by the shoulders and started to shake me so hard I feared my teeth would fall out of my head. My father began to shout at my mother to stop and Jane stood by, laughing.

And so we did not notice the Doctor arrive, or see him bend down over the rope-walker. But we heard him say, "While you argue, this boy suffers."

The sound of his voice brought my mother to her senses. At once Jane and I were instructed to bring the rope-walker in. To take him to the room my father used as a study and which had a truckle bed in it. For he sometimes worked late into the night.

"When he is made comfortable," the Doctor said, "I will take a look at him."

This was the first time I had seen the Doctor after our meeting at the Head and Combe. Since then he had appeared in my mind's eye as larger than life and as wickedly seductive as sin. It was a shock to see him play the Good Samaritan.

"We will pay you for your trouble, of course," said my father hurriedly.

But the Doctor would not hear of it. "It was Margrat who thought to bring him home," he said.

How had he known that? Had he shadowed me? "I merely follow her example."

It was cleverly done. A compliment to me and to my mother, for having borne such a tender-hearted daughter. I had been many times to the theatre with my father. I ought to have seen the trick of it. But I confess I was unaware of how he set the stage.

He must have noticed the rope-walker's ring when he first bent down to look at him. But he said nothing at first. He waited. His display of charity only increased his reputation in my father and mother's eyes. And I confess it now… in mine too.

Once the rope-walker was safely tucked in bed, the Doctor sent Jane out to the apothecary's for a sleeping draught. "Sleep is a great healer. When he awakes, I will examine him and see if there is anything to be done."

I thought it was strange that the Doctor did not attend to him directly, but I said nothing. As to my mother, all she cared about was that the Doctor still had time to eat dinner with us.

So while the rope-walker slept, the Doctor took pains to charm my mother and father. He complimented my mother's fine cooking and my father's choice of wines.

He talked about his travels in Egypt, and said, with the utmost delicacy, that there was much money to be made from the trade in Egyptian artefacts. He invited them to call on him in his house in the Strand and see the many treasures he had there.

"Though I fear," he said, with a modest smile, "you will find fault with the housekeeping as I have no wife to look to it."

I fixed my eyes on my plate and did not look up. But I flushed the deepest red.

"Margrat will make someone a good wife," my mother said quickly, causing me to wish the earth might suddenly open up and swallow me whole. "If they have no objection to the colour of her hair."

"I think it very beautiful, on her at least. But now..." He pushed back his chair and threw his napkin on the table, saying, "I must go and see how the boy does."

My mother led the Doctor to the study. My father and I followed on. Jane had been sent to the kitchen to fetch hot water and clean towels.

The rope-walker was still asleep. Though his face was caked in dried blood and the purple of a bruise bloomed across his left temple, he looked peaceful. His right hand pillowed his cheek.

The Doctor bent over him. I held my breath. I was sure that he would see the ring now. Would he whisper to the rope-walker the very same thing he had whispered to me?

He did not, saying only, "Boy, wake up now, I have come to examine you."

The rope-walker must have journeyed a long way in his dreams, for he came to very slowly. At first he did not know where he was. He shouted and tried to jump from the bed, pushing the Doctor out of the way. But the Doctor caught him by the wrist and held him. Now I saw that he was looking at the rope-walker's ring. He smiled, but so fleetingly I wondered if I had seen it at all. Then he said, with a voice as sharp as flint, "The boy must be turned out of the house this instant."

The shock of it. As if a link boy, lighting my way home, had turned and stabbed me with a knife.

"Why? What is the matter? Does he show signs of the plague?" My father backed slowly towards the door, pulling me with him.

"Worse," said the Doctor. "Much worse."

"What could be worse than that?" said my mother,

clutching a hand to her mouth.

"The plague attacks only the body," said the Doctor. "The sickness this boy carries with him attacks the very soul itself."

My mother gasped, made the sign of the cross and muttered a quick prayer under her breath.

"See this ring he wears? I have seen it before…" The Doctor was looking straight at me and I held my breath, for now I would be undone. My father would know I was a thief and I would be severely punished. "It is worn by the members of a secret sect; followers of an Ancient Egyptian goddess called Sekhmet. Wherever her disciples go, plague and pestilence follow."

My mother cried, "I will call the constable and have him arrested this minute."

Then she was gone and missed what followed after. For the rope-walker, hearing her words, struggled to escape. I saw the colour drain from his face with the pain, but fear of capture drove him on.

Though the Doctor still had hold of his arm, the ropewalker now leaped from the bed. He pushed past my father, past Jane, spilling her jug of hot water, out through the front door and into the street. We ran after, but he was too quick for us.

"No matter," said my father. "If he has any sense

he will lie low for a while and then leave London."

I could see from the Doctor's expression that he did not believe it. "I hope that you are right, but you must keep a close watch on Margrat. For the sect preys on young girls with red hair and plucks them straight from the street. They disappear and are never seen again."

"For what purpose?" I asked, the words as faint as a mouse's breath.

The Doctor said nothing. His silence hung in the air between us, as eloquent as any words. I was imagining a fate far worse than any he could have described.

Chapter 6

Claire knew her mum was bubbling over with suppressed rage. And she knew why. That man, Robert Benoit, had clearly wanted to buy the box the minute he'd stepped into the house and seen it. Had offered, before he left, a great deal of money, if only they would sell it to him. But Claire had kept a tight hold on the box, even though her ring wouldn't open it. She wasn't going to give it up. However much her mum had pleaded and threatened. So he'd gone away empty-handed.

Now her mum didn't know what to do with all her anger and was so charged up that she was going through the house like a whirlwind. Wearing only a halter-necked top and a pair of shorts and with her hair pulled up in a clip, she was stripping shelves bare and emptying cupboards. Out in the street a skip was already piled high with stuff. It didn't seem as if anything could stop her. Not even the heat.

Scorching, even in the shade and no sign of it easing up and everything starting to shrivel up and die.

Then there were the rats. There had only been one at first. But out in broad daylight and running along the garden wall and pushing through a gap hardly bigger than a thumb's width, into the brick outhouse next to the kitchen.

Claire's mum had been in the garden, ripping out weeds. She'd looked up and seen it and had screamed so loudly Claire and Micky had heard it and come running. All the way down from the attic, where they'd been looking through a box of old trains and track.

* * *

The next time there had been two rats. One of them really big. Black and sleek, with a long grey tail as fat as a twist of rope. They had run across the grass and swarmed up onto the bird table, where they sat eating sunflower seeds like two ugly great birds.

Claire's mum had been washing up at the kitchen sink and ran out, still wearing pink rubber gloves and banging on a saucepan lid with a wooden spoon. They'd scurried away. But it wasn't long before they were back. And this time there were three.

Her mum had rung the council at once. But the line was always engaged. And then when she did get through, they said there would be a two-week wait before anyone could come out. They'd been snowed under with calls. There was a plague of rats. *Black* rats, which was very unusual. Maybe the hot summer had encouraged them to breed.

So all they could do was wait and watch and listen. Every little noise sent them into a panic. Claire lay awake at night imagining rats running over the bed and across her face. Claire's mum said they must keep the toilet lid closed and weighed down with the 2lb weight from the kitchen scales. She'd heard they could swim up the U-bends in toilets.

Only Micky didn't seem scared, telling her mum that it was okay because black rats didn't like swimming as much as brown ones. And after that, at every mealtime, she told them a new rat fact: they had 'collapsible' bones that meant they could squeeze through the smallest of gaps. That no one was ever more than two metres away from one.

That they could breed at a phenomenal rate and had litters of anything from six to eleven babies, up to five times a year. (Claire silently did the maths and shuddered.) Oh… and they were carriers of typhus, plague and a type of parasite that could infect your body and slowly kill you. And it was fleas carried by *black* rats that had spread the Great Plague of 1665.

Now there were black rats on the streets again and another type of plague just beginning. And Claire knew it was no coincidence.

* * *

"Do you think they can spread bird flu, too? Or is that just chickens?" Claire asked. She was watching the six o'clock news on the television.

Two hundred cases of bird flu reported in London now and spreading. Hospitals were starting to feel the strain. Anyone flying in from Hong Kong or the Far East was facing stringent medical examinations. But it was all too little and too late, because it was already here.

The Chief Medical Officer was urging everyone to remain calm. But on the tube and on trains and buses, people had started to wear masks. And when a woman collapsed on the escalator in a big London store, there had been panic and two people injured in the rush to get away. It had turned out that she was pregnant and had simply fainted in the heat.

"Poor thing. I hope the baby was okay," Claire's mum had said, looking pale. Claire had looked up in surprise; had been expecting her to say, "Stupid woman. Pregnant and shopping in all this heat."

"Well I hope Dad's being careful, that's all," Claire said. He was away on business. Dublin this time. He'd said he would call if he could, but they hadn't heard from him for over a week now and as usual his mobile was switched off.

"What did you expect?" said Claire's mum, when Claire moaned about it. "Once he's gone, he never thinks about us at all. He never has. Out of sight. Out of mind." She stopped. "We could be dead for all he'd know or care."

Then she turned and ran out of the room and Claire knew she was crying. And she hadn't even done that when Grandma had died.

* * *

Claire lay awake for a long time that night thinking about death. She even crept out of bed and tiptoed across the room to check that Micky was still breathing. Leaning in close to her; stroking her bare arm, until, making tiny, snuffling animal noises, Micky surfaced just long enough to shake Claire's hand away and turn on her side. Claire watched as she curled up, drawing her arms and legs and head in, like a little sleeping dormouse. Her shock of brown hair, fringed black with sweat and the nibbed ridge of her curving spine, just visible in the light from the moon outside.

Suppose something happened to her mum? Or what if they all died and it was just her left? What then? Where would she go? Now Grandma was dead, there was no one else. Only a few distant cousins and she was sure they wouldn't want her.

I'll be 14 soon, she thought. *And then I'll be able to look after myself.*

But she didn't believe it. And when she did finally fall asleep her dreams were vivid and disturbing. Her mum and Micky were inside the house and she was locked out. She ran round, banging frantically on all the doors and windows. Trying desperately to attract their attention; warn them that something terrible was going to happen. But they didn't seem to hear her, because they were talking and laughing with that man. Robert. With his long dark hair and his hungry eyes and everything about him distorted, as if she was looking at him through a twisted mirror. *He* heard her though, because he turned towards her and smiled and she stopped banging and in the silence that followed, she heard him say quite clearly, but inside her head, "You are bound to me now and will be for ever." The words repeating themselves, as if they were playing over and over again on a loop. And all the while, rivulets of rats running around and over her feet.

When she woke up the next morning, the dream stayed with her, vivid and terrifying still.

Maybe, she thought, *if I tell Mum about it, I'll be able to forget it.*

So she went to find her. But she was in Grandma's study, busy emptying out drawers in the mahogany desk that stood in the front bay window and didn't see the look on Claire's face as she talked about it… or register the fear in her voice.

"Think, Claire," she was saying. "How surprising is it that he was in your dream? And the rats. And me and Micky. Not surprising at all really. I've been having some…" She stopped what she was saying to bend over and pull out a roll of paper from the bottom right-hand drawer. "Now I wonder what this is… your grandma had so much stuff you wouldn't believe. Masses and masses of cuttings about plague outbreaks all over the world. And not to mention all the stuff on circuses. I mean, how weird is that?"

Claire didn't think it was weird at all. Not now anyway, because it didn't seem to her that her grandma had ever done anything without a purpose. But Claire had no idea what the purpose was. She could understand all the plague stuff. But circuses, tightrope walkers. Where did they fit in to the puzzle?

"Can I have these?" Claire unclipped the circus tickets. Held them out for her mum to look at. "Only it IS my birthday soon and Jade says she'll come with me. If you go early you can join in, do a workshop. Jade would love that."

"You hate circuses! Anyway, I don't want you going Claire. Not now. Not with the flu. You shouldn't be going to crowded places. And I don't want to catch it."

For a second her mum seemed flustered. So

Claire pocketed the tickets quickly while she wasn't paying attention.

"Now…" Claire's mum had pulled herself together and was clearing a space on the desktop and smoothing out the roll of paper. "Oh… the famous family tree. Well I suppose I'd better keep it. Though why anyone would be interested in a load of dead people is beyond me."

But Claire was interested, because at the top of the tree she could see a name. Margrat Jennet. Born 23rd December 1651. She did a quick count in her head. So she would have turned 14 in 1665, the year of the Plague.

My age, she thought, *give or take a few weeks. And was it the same name she'd struggled to read on the manuscript? She knew it was.*

"Can I have it? I'll look after it."

"If you want."

But not the box. She couldn't have that, because it might be valuable. And this wasn't. Just names.

She left her mum clearing out the rest of the desk drawers and she took the family tree upstairs to Grandma's bedroom, where there was space to spread it out on the floor in front of the bay window.

She knelt down and unrolled it, weighting down the corners with four books she pulled off a nearby shelf. Then she bent over to study it.

There at the top, Margrat Jennet, born in the parish of St Lawrence Jewry. There at the bottom, her own name, with her date of birth, the 7th August. Beside Margrat's name, Grandma had written 'red hair' and underlined it. And beside Claire's name, she'd written the same. And why was that fact important enough for her to have underlined it? She traced all the names down, noticing with surprise that all the children born who had survived, were girls. All the boys had been still-born or died shortly after birth. And no one else was listed as having red hair. And how on earth did Grandma know that Margrat had? And why was it important enough for her to underline it?

Claire sat back on her heels and rubbed the palms of her hands dry on her shorts.

She felt a little quiver of excitement at the thought of a connection made across three hundred and fifty years and ten generations to this Margrat Jennet, who was her direct ancestor! What had she looked like? *Anything like me?*

Claire jumped up and ran to look in the

dressing-table mirror. Did the face that stared back look anything like Margrat's? Were Margrat's eyes that changeable colour too? Sometimes grey. Sometimes green.

Maybe they were, she thought. Maybe I'm a throwback.

So many questions and would the sheaf of papers that Grandma had left with the ring hold the answers? All she had to do was be brave. Stop thinking that stupid nonsense about the plague and take the papers and try and decipher the writing. Surely the ring and the papers and the box were all connected? She could go and fetch the papers now. But the thought of it still scared her – she felt stupid – but it did.

She would move back into Grandma's bedroom *tomorrow* and then look at the papers properly. Late at night when she wouldn't be disturbed. Good, she felt better now she'd made that decision. And if it was too hard and she struggled to read them, then she would find someone to help her. Someone who knew about 17th century writing. Someone at the university, where her dad was currently working on some complicated IT project. Maybe she should save time and do that anyway. Now.

She fetched her mobile. Took it into the loo and locked the door. Best not to let her mum know she was ringing Dad. Even mentioning his name these days made her angry.

She keyed in his number. It rang out, but there was no reply. She left a message, "I need to speak to you Dad. As soon as you get back. Ring me. Please."

Now Micky was banging on the door. "Claire. I'm going to pee my pants if you don't come out now."

Claire sighed, locked her phone and slipped it into her jeans pocket. Then she flushed the toilet and unlocked the door, hoping that her dad would ring back that minute.

But he didn't call until the next morning when her mum and Micky were out.

"I'm in Dublin until tomorrow," he said. "Only just picked up your message. Sorry. It's been so busy, there hasn't been a minute…"

Not even a minute to think about your daughter?

"Dad, can you do something for me when you get back? Please, and I need you not to tell Mum about it."

"Well…"

"Grandma left me something. An old manuscript. It was written in the 17th century. But the writing's all scratchy and blotchy and I can't work it out. I need someone to help me translate it. Please, please."

"Why can't you ask your mum?"

Why couldn't she? Because the minute Mum knew about it she'd tell that man and it was somehow important that he didn't know. But Claire couldn't explain that to her dad, so she pretended not to have heard the question.

"Please... please. There'll be someone at the university won't there? Someone you could ask?"

"Maybe..."

"Can you call round tomorrow, on your way back from the airport? It's on your way. Say yes."

"I don't know. It might be awkward, Claire. I don't think I want to see your mum right now."

"You don't have to. You can park down the road and ring me and I'll come out with it. She won't even have to know that you're here."

"All right. But make sure that she doesn't. And Micky. Don't bring Micky." He rang off.

Good, thought Claire. But then a little worry started to niggle away at her. Supposing the papers got lost somewhere in the university. Maybe she should photocopy them and give her dad the copies. Yes, she would do that. Now. Before her mum came back. There was a copy shop in the High Street on the other side of the common. Her mum had used it to copy papers to do with Grandma's will.

So she went into the kitchen, opened the dresser drawer and took out the envelope. She hesitated. *I'll just hand them the envelope,* she thought, *and say, "Copy the papers inside please." And I won't even have to touch them.* She steeled herself. Slid her fingers inside the envelope. Registered the dry, crackling, whispering sound as she pulled the papers half out. Struggled still to read the first few lines. But Margrat's name leaped out clear now. She found she could make out a few of the other words too. Saying them out loud helped her decipher them, "My name is Margrat Jennet. I live now in the house of Nicholas Robert Benedict, physician. My mother and father are both dead. I live in fear…"

She felt her heartbeat falter and for a minute she couldn't catch her breath. She was shaking as she pushed the papers hurriedly back inside the envelope. And she was still shaking as she stuffed the envelope into her backpack and went out of the door, down the road and across the common.

* * *

She'd been going to look at the papers again, now that she'd had them photocopied. And she had looked at the photocopies later when she was in bed and alone. Had made out a few more words and sentences. But the effort of it had made her feel so tired, she'd fallen asleep and when she'd opened her eyes again it was the next morning. So she decided she would wait now until she had the translation… typed out on clean, fresh, uncontaminated paper. And maybe that wouldn't take too long, because her dad had just rung her mobile and said, "I'm turning into the road. I can see a space at the end by the postbox. I'll stop there."

She listened carefully. She could hear the wheezing hum of the vacuum cleaner. Her mum was cleaning furiously still. And she knew Micky was upstairs, playing with the train set. She had the track snaking all around her room and she was busy making station buildings out of cereal boxes.

Claire pulled her clothes on quickly, picked up the photocopies sealed in a big brown envelope with her name and Grandma's address on it, and tiptoed downstairs. Putting the front door on the catch, she slipped out.

* * *

"Dad!"

He was standing next to the car, leaning against it. His tie was loose. His shirtsleeves were rolled up. He looked hot and tired. "Who's my best girl?" He gave her a hug. Lifted her off her feet. A faint odour of sweat, the plastic smell of planes and airports and the sharp scent of an aftershave she didn't recognise. "Now what's this you want me to do?"

It was then that she noticed there was someone sitting in the car. A woman. Short dark hair framing a thin angular face. Not pretty, but young. Younger than Dad anyway. Younger than her mum.

He saw Claire looking, but when she looked back at him, his eyes slid away from hers and he pretended he hadn't noticed. "Is this it?" He held out his hand for the envelope. "Can't promise I'll get anyone to do it. But I'll try. Right. Must be off." He gave her a kiss on the cheek. Got back in the car and waved a hand out of the open window as he pulled away.

The woman in the passenger seat turned her head to look back. She was smiling.

Claire stood totally still for a moment, watching until the car had turned the corner and was gone. Then she walked slowly back towards the house, the sun full on her face, making her screw up her eyes, so the tears were squeezed out and trickled down, cool against her hot skin. Spoke sharply and out loud to herself. "Stupid cow. What are you crying for?"

Wiped both cheeks roughly with the back of her hand and as soon as she was indoors, she went up to Grandma's room, closing the door quietly and carefully behind her. She wanted to be alone to think about what this might mean. Another woman? Did her mum know? Would she care anyway, because *she* had left *him*? Or... and this wasn't something she'd thought about before... was that *why* she'd left him?

She went and lay on the bed, face down, feeling

the cool silk of the bedspread on her cheek and the palms of her hands. She didn't want to think about her dad with someone else. Someone younger. Her mind raced ahead. She saw her dad with another family and forgetting all about her and Micky. And the thought caused her a real physical pain, which rippled out until her fingertips ached with it. And if she felt like this, how must her mum be feeling, really?

It would explain a lot of things.

Oh God, she thought, *how easy it is to get things wrong*. Misjudge people, misread their motives for doing things. Maybe her mum wasn't as cold and selfish as she thought. Maybe Grandma hadn't been either. Claire sighed. Well it was too late to be nicer to Grandma, but she could be much kinder to her mum. Maybe the manuscript was somehow a key to that. Maybe that was why Grandma had left it for her. Well, as long as her dad found someone to look at it, maybe she would soon know.

Manuscript 6

Fearing that, as the Doctor had warned, I might be plucked from the street by the sect and never seen again, my mother would not let me out of her sight... even to stand on the doorstep to take the air! But after a while she grew careless. There were errands to run and when Jane tripped and hurt her ankle, no one to run them. So one morning, in late March, she sent me out alone to the candlemaker's. I was pleased, for I was tired of being confined to the house or the shop and always in the company of my mother, or father, or Jane.

It was true that the Doctor was a frequent and welcome visitor to the house; always arriving unexpectedly and at any time of the day or evening, catching me off guard and causing my heart to beat fast and my hands to tremble. But we were never alone for more than a few moments, before my mother, hearing his voice, was there with us.

Once he had asked if he might take me to visit the menagerie at the Tower. But my mother said she had never been there and so came with us. If the Doctor — now he said we must call him Nicholas — was vexed, he didn't show it, though I was very cross. In truth he seemed pleased, paying my mother a great deal of attention the whole day.

I thought she would never stop talking of it. If a chicken had cackled so much, I would have quickly wrung its neck.

I made my way up Sopers Lane. The weather was mild and sunny. There was a lightness in my step at the unexpected freedom. A smile on my face as I stopped by the baker's and breathed in the rich heady smell of meat pies. I bought one, ate it and was already licking my fingers clean as I turned in to Toure Roual. The streets were crowded. Everyone was in high spirits, bustling and loud. So at first I did not notice that I was being followed. Even then I saw no one. It was more a prickling of the hairs at the back of my neck. A shiver passing down my spine. The day seemed suddenly colder. The voice of the crowd now shrill and harsh.

Several times I stopped all of a sudden and spun round, but saw nothing strange. I had just started to *breathe more easily; was walking down past the church of St John's and was nearly at my destination, when a hand reached out and I was roughly pulled into the stinking, fetid blackness of a nearby alley.*

I felt a rat brush against the hem of my skirt and run over my foot. I began to scream, but no sound came out, for a hand was pressed against my mouth. A voice I knew said, "Do not be afraid. I will not hurt you, but you must listen to me, for you are in grave danger."

As if I did not know that already. And I meant to flee from it and him, as soon as I was able. But he pinned my arms to my side and held me fast. "It is I, Christophe. The rope-walker you took pity on."

I was struggling hard now, but though he was not much taller than me, he was a great deal stronger.

I fought as desperately as any cat tied up in a sack and tried to bite his hand.

"The ring you wear on a braid about your neck..."

I grew still. I felt his grip loosen and he took his hand from my mouth. I was able to twist round. My eyes had grown accustomed to the dark and I could see his face, just a breath away from mine.

"When you found it..."

He knew. How?

"Were there other things... scrolls... a casket? An emerald-green casket?"

"My father gave me the ring, for my 13th birthday. The 23rd day of December, in the year of our Lord 1664." A lie, but I thought such detail would make him believe me. "I know nothing about any scrolls."

More lies, but I had promised the Doctor I would tell no one about them. How was it this boy knew of them? The rope-walker frowned.

"Or any casket?"

That at least was true. The Doctor had said nothing about a casket. And if it had come into the shop with the scrolls, then I should have seen it.

"But the Doctor knows that you have the ring?"

"He does," I said, for what harm could come of telling him that? "He... Nicholas, said that I must keep it always about me, for it would protect me from the plague. But that I should never wear it on my finger..."

I reached for the ring now, but the rope-walker took my hand and held it tight. "But as long as he does not have the Emerald Casket, then all is not lost." His eyes glittered with such ferocious intensity that I shrank away from him and tried to pull my hand free. "Listen.

What I have to tell you... when my father first told me, I did not believe it." He looked quickly around. His voice had sunk to an urgent whisper. "I am a rope-walker. My father was a rope-walker and his father before him. Once, a very long time ago, our ancestors lived in Egypt, where they were both feared and worshipped for the colour of their hair. Not as pure a red as yours, but red still. They were priests and priestesses at the Temple of the Lady of Red Linen, the goddess Sekhmet."

"And you are her servant still and Nicholas is right, you are wicked...."

"Not a servant, Margrat. A guardian. Of a great secret. My father told me that the ring he wore on the third finger of his right hand was special; twin to a ring that was the key to unlocking the most powerful spell in the world. In truth, I did not believe him. Then one day, late in September, three years past, we stopped in the square of a little town outside Paris. We set up the poles and the rope, and when a small crowd had gathered, my father started his walk. You must be master of your thoughts to do it or you will slip. My father was such a master. I had never seen him fall. But that day was different. All of a sudden he stopped and stood quite still. Then he began pulling on

the ring. He looked as if he was listening to a voice that only he could hear. He hurried to jump down... slipped, and fell. He lay there on the cobbles, in terrible pain, unable to move, while the crowd pressed in around us. I knelt beside him. His hand, wearing the ring, reached up and pulled me down so my ear was close to his mouth. Then he told me the story of the scrolls. How they contain all the knowledge and wisdom of the great god Thoth."

I held my breath.

"How the first 20 scrolls contain powerful spells. Whoever recites them can keep sickness and death at bay. But it is the 21st spell that is the most powerful of all. So it was placed inside an emerald casket, made from a substance unknown to alchemy. And to keep it safe, a young red-haired girl called Nefertaru, a dancer at the Temple of Sekhmet, was chosen to wear the key... which took the form of a ring. And only she could carry the casket and the spells, safe into the afterlife..."

Nefertaru! And now her mummy was on show for all to see.

"If that were true and she had carried them safe into the afterlife," I said, thinking I had found the flaw in his logic, "then how is it that you believe the Doctor

has the spells and I wear Nefertaru's ring....?" But then, all at once, I remembered what the Doctor had said. That the door to the afterlife had been locked tight against her, because someone had written NefARtaru and not NefERtaru. And I could have told Christophe that... but I kept my mouth shut.

"I only know what my father told me... that she was buried with them in a tomb deep under the floor of Sekhmet's temple and the tomb was watched over by guardians, each wearing a ring bearing the same hieroglyphics as Nefertaru's. Not keys to the casket, yet rings with great power. But time passed. The Temple of Sekhmet fell into ruin. The guardians, exiled from Egypt, became rope-walkers, jugglers, acrobats, scattered across the world. If there were other guardians still wearing their rings, then my father did not know of them, but our ring had been passed down faithfully through our family, the eldest in each generation wearing it. One day, my father believed, the 21st spell would be in danger and a 'guardian' would be called upon to help save it. For should the spells and the Emerald Casket ever fall into the wrong hands, the ring would tell the guardian. There would be a sign."

"How can any ring do that?" I said scornfully.

"I did not believe it either. But with his dying

breath, my father told me to take his ring, which slipped easily then from his finger, and put it on. So I did. 'Does it burn?' he whispered, clutching at my shirt and pulling me in close. 'Mon dieu, how it burned. That is the sign and you must heed the prophecy:

> *He who loves wickedness*
> *Cloaks himself in the odour of sanctity.*
> *At his coming will be great plagues.*

> *He seeks the one who holds the key to life,*
> *The true daughter and the red-haired maiden.*

> *When she is found, then all will hear*
> *Thoth's mighty voice*
> *And the wicked shall be made small as dust*
> *Before the storm.'*

At first I did not understand what it meant..." Christophe faltered.

But I saw at once what it signified. That it was psalms from the Bible *joined and twisted and turned upon their heads and I began to say,* "It is not Nicholas *who loves wickedness..."*

But Christophe's hand stopped my mouth. "My father

told me 'Follow where the plague leads and let the ring guide you.' So I did, to Egypt, then to Alexandria and the Doctor, who was well known there. Seeing my ring, he knew at once that I had come for the spells and the casket and he fled from me. I followed and found him again in London, but the ring stayed loose on my finger. It did not tighten and burn as it had before. I did not know what that signified and I was at a loss to know what I should do next. I feared I had failed my father. Then, knocked down from the rope and beaten by the mob, you saved me. I did not even have to open my eyes and look at you to know you wore Nefertaru's ring. For I felt my ring tighten and burn on my finger, the minute you came close. Then I looked up and saw the colour of your hair..."

Now there was silence. Did he really wish me to believe that I was the red-haired maiden? That I held the key to the greatest spell on earth? Who was it that told the truth? Nicholas or this rope-walker? If one of them was wicked, which one was it? It did not seem in the least clear, for in many ways I was my parents' child. Raised by my father to have respect for men of learning and by my mother to have none for those who were poor and lived on their wits.

Appearances. I knew that they could deceive.

That a man might seem compassionate and kind and yet be wicked to his core. For that is how the Devil works in this world. He seeks out our weaknesses and uses them to trap us into sin. I had been told it was so many times. And I had many weaknesses. For one, I told myself that I was seduced by Nicholas's fine words and clever talk; his reputation and wealth. But in my heart I knew it was something much darker than that. Something I had no word for as yet. But I felt it when he came close. It made my breathing quicken. It made me feel I was drowning and glad of it. I thought that if he should even brush his hand against mine, my whole body would be flooded with a pain so exquisite, I would be ready to endure it for all eternity. Though I feared the strength of these feelings, I had never wanted anything in my life so badly before. So, I turned to Christophe, saying, "Go away. Leave me alone. I cannot help you. Nicholas... the Doctor... is a well-respected man. You are just a boy, a nothing, a prancer on a rope." I pushed past him and he did not try to stop me. I walked fast along Cheapside towards the candlemaker's and I did not once look back.

But I thought about the meeting constantly. When Nicholas called later that day, I studied him intently. I saw that he made sure I was close by when he said to my father, "I was surprised, John," (Such intimate terms, though I noticed that my father, in deference to the Doctor's status, did not call him by his first name.) "to see Margrat come out from the candlemaker's this morning and all alone."

Had he seen me then, with Christophe?

I watched as my father's face coloured up and he started to bluster. He turned to my mother, who, always happy to tell a lie if it made her life more comfortable, said "Sir. Shame on you. Would we risk the life of our only daughter?"

There was the briefest of silences. It was clear that Nicholas did not doubt that she would.

She held his gaze brazenly and to my great surprise, he looked away first, saying, "I apologise, Catherine, for I must be in error."

A triumph then for my mother, but in truth not much of one. For we all knew that Nicholas had not been mistaken and was really the victor. From that day on, I was never allowed out alone again.

But I was not the only one who would grow wild at such close confinement. For the plague was growing worse by the day.

In early April, a fiery comet lit up the sky, causing

fear and dread, for it was a clear omen of evil and a portent of sickness.

At first, though, there was only a trickle of deaths; a smattering of houses closed up. (And those to the west of where we lived, in the parishes of St Giles-in-the-Fields, St Martin and St Clement Danes.) We felt safe.

But by July, the ripples from the flood of deaths lapped at our toes. Searchers, examiners, watchmen and nurses were appointed to seek out, diagnose, care for and confine those dying of the plague. Their houses were to be marked with a cross and none allowed to leave them. Entertainments of any sort were prohibited. No beggars, players, jugglers or rope-walkers were allowed in the streets.

That is good, I thought. Christophe will have left the city and I need not think on him again. Yet I did think of him. Would I ever see him again? But though my bedroom window looked out over the lane and I spent a great deal of time looking out, I never did catch a glimpse of him… at least not from there.

Chapter Seven

When Claire went downstairs the next morning, her head still muzzy with sleep, she found her mum and Micky already in the kitchen. They were frantically emptying out the larder where the food was kept. Everything except stuff in tins was going into black plastic bags.

"Rats!" Her mum was looking hot and frazzled. Packets of flour, sugar, cereals, pasta, all with great big holes gnawed in the side and their contents cascading out onto the floor. "They've even had a go at eating this!" She held up a white candle from the emergency supply, kept in case of power cuts.

Micky took it from her and looked at it closely. "Wow! Big teeth marks! Did you know rats can eat their way through bricks and even concrete? And…"

"Shut up Micky! It's no good. I can't wait for those pest-control men any longer. I'm going out to see if I can get any rat traps. *If* there *are* any. It said on the news that this rat plague is getting worse by the day. And then I'd better go to the supermarket and get some more food. Maybe even one of those squidgy chocolate cakes for your sister's birthday. And if we keep it in the fridge, the rats won't get it! What do you think Micky? Shall we? I don't suppose you're going to want to come and help though, are you Claire?"

Claire shook her head. She was still in the old T-shirt and shorts she wore as pyjamas.

But Micky said, "I'll come!" and ran off to put on shoes. Sweets. She was planning on coming back with masses of sweets.

* * *

Her mum and Micky had only just gone when the doorbell went. Thinking it was Micky running back to fetch her purse, which she'd carelessly left on the bottom step of the stairs, she opened the door. But it wasn't Micky. It was that man.

She tried to keep calm. She took a step back behind the door and kept her hand firmly on it, ready to slam it shut. She wasn't going to let him in.

"Sorry, you've just missed my mum. You'll have to come back another time." She waited for a split-second, thinking he would say something and when he didn't, she started to close the door. Something made her stop. What was it? The way he was looking at her with such fierce intensity? It seemed as if he wanted to draw her in and hold her fast there. But she wouldn't let him and broke free of his gaze and then he seemed to sag and lean heavily on his walking stick. As if all the life was draining out of him. His skin looked sallow. His eyes glittered. Sweat was beading his top lip. All at once he looked old and sick and frail. No threat at all.

"Are you feeling okay? Do you want to come in and sit down for a moment?" The very second she'd said the words, she wished she hadn't, because his shoulders went back and he drew himself up tall, as if the sickness and frailty had just been an act. She thought she saw a look of triumph in his eyes and her heart skipped a beat. She hesitated. It was still not too late to shut the door, but then, in a flash, he had slipped past her, becoming just a shadowy figure in the darkness of the hall.

"This is very kind of you," he said and the sound

of his voice was powerfully hypnotic. Her grip on reality faded. His voice seemed to be whispering in her ear, over and over: *You are mine now and always will be.*

Then the rattle and thud of post being pushed through the letterbox and falling to the hall floor and the sound of it brought her to her senses.

I'll make him leave, she thought. But too late, the kitchen door was wide open and when she went in, there he was, sitting at the table. The black bag was at his feet and he had taken off his jacket, folded it carefully and placed it on his knee. He was leaning back, resting his head against the wall, his eyes closed. His skin looked unnaturally white; the colour of bleached flour.

"Sorry," he said, his eyes still closed. "It's the heat. I find it drains all the life out of me. You'd think I'd be used to it after all this time." His eyes snapped open and he looked straight at her.

There was something about his voice, his accent. What was it?

"London has always been unbearable in the heat. Humid. Oppressive. The heat in Egypt is very different."

"You don't come from Egypt, do you?" she

asked. Maybe that was it. Maybe he'd lived abroad for so long his accent had changed.

"Oh, no. I know Egypt well, but I come from London and I've lived in the same house for what seems like for ever." He smiled.

She found herself smiling back and asking, "Do you want some tea? Black, with no sugar, isn't it?" She'd remembered.

Claire watched as he cradled the cup in his hands. He closed his eyes as he drank and she couldn't help studying his face; noticing the small dark mole, high up on his left cheek, in exactly the same place she had hers.

"Well, I suppose I should go now," he said, putting the cup carefully down on its saucer, "Please tell your mother I'll call her. Tell her I will pay handsomely for the box."

Claire felt a curious conflict of emotions as he said that. Fear. Then a sudden bright, inexplicable flame of excitement flaring up, but quickly dying away again.

He stood up and put on his jacket. He picked up his black bag and stick. Claire started for the door, but he was ahead of her. She was flustered to find herself squeezing past him through the doorway. There was something frightening about having him that close. And that smell again. The cinnamon and flowers.

At the front door he stopped and said, as if he had only just thought of it, "No, even better. Ask your mother to come and have tea with me. Next Friday at three o'clock. And you must come too of course. And Micky."

"Not Friday," she said sharply. "Friday's my birthday."

"Well, Thursday then. I'll make sure we have a special cake… with 14 candles. And I think you'll find my house very interesting. Full of things I've collected over the years."

Fourteen. How had he known that? And not an invitation, Claire thought. *Much more an instruction.* As if he had no doubts at all that they would all go. And while he was there, standing so close to her, she had no doubt that she would go, either. She wanted to go. Why wouldn't she?

It was only once he had gone. When she had closed the door behind him and was leaning against it, pressing her forehead against the cool glass, that she felt the fear bubbling up again. As if, any moment now, something really terrible and unexpected was going to happen.

Manuscript 7

Many left the city as the plague grew worse; packing all their belongings onto carts and in carriages if they could afford them, or onto any riverboats still plying their trade.

At first my mother had not wanted to leave, fearing the house would be broken into and looted in our absence. My father, likewise, worried that all his books and manuscripts would be stolen from the shop. But the death toll grew so alarming, my mother became more hysterical by the day. Her fear was infectious. Jane left us, packing her few belongings and stealing away in the night. Now there was no one else to risk sending out into the streets to buy food. My mother begged my father to leave and I believe he would have done, if it had not been for Nicholas.

"I promise, you will be quite safe staying here. Take two spoonfuls of my Plague Water every time you step out of the house," he said, giving them a brown *glass bottle of foul-smelling amber liquid. "And carry these with you at all times." He held out two dark wax figures. Tiny dolls that had strands of dull red hair stuck to their heads and fragments of papyrus pushed into a slit in their backs. "Without them and the Plague Water, I would surely have died in Egypt."*

So they faithfully took the medicine as prescribed and carried the amulets Nicholas had given them. Believing themselves to be thus protected from infection, they went out: my father to his shop (though there was little trade; the only books and manuscripts offered, surely stolen from abandoned houses) and my mother to find food.

I stayed at home. At first all seemed well, though my father came home saying the shop had been broken into and looted.

And my mother came home with terrible tales of babies found still sucking at the breasts of their dead mothers. Of men and women senseless with grief. Of sinners driven mad with terror at the thought they might die and with their sins not absolved.

"Oh," she said, "and the stink!"

Even though I kept to the house, the smell seeped in. The stench of rotting corpses, human excrement and rubbish. For as more and more people died, there were fewer left to bury the dead, empty the lay stalls or sweep the streets. And now that all the cats and dogs had been ordered destroyed, rats ran everywhere unchecked. It was as if the city itself was one great weeping sore.

Then in the dog days of August, my father began to feel ill. He complained of an aching head that grew steadily worse. He lost all interest in food and what little he drank was vomited straight back up again.

Now his head ached so ferociously, he lay doubled up in pain on the parlour floor and nothing we could do soothed him. His face was quite drained of colour and was filmed with sweat. His eyes glittered. His lips were parched and cracked. His tongue was swollen. All signs of the plague, except one. There was no ring of roses. No red swellings.

"It cannot be the plague," said my mother, her voice quite calm. "For the amulets and medicine protect us." Her belief in Nicholas was absolute. "And if it is not the plague, your father must have some other sickness and we might all catch it. Margrat, I cannot leave your father and there is no one else I can trust to go. You must hurry to the Doctor's house. If he is at home… and I pray that he is… then ask him to come at once. We need his help or your father will surely die. If you should happen to meet with anyone on the way,

do not tell them your father is sick, or the searcher will come. The house will be shut up and all will be lost."

I had never been to Nicholas's house, in spite of all his promises, nor had my mother, though she had asked about it and knew where it was: outside of the City walls and set back a little from the Strand.

It was getting late, past seven o'clock, but I set out at once. If I hurried I would be sure to get there and back before nightfall. Though the heat was terrible, I stepped out, cloaked and hooded and carrying a posy of the sweetest-smelling flowers from the garden. But nothing was proof against the stench of the streets. It grew worse in the warren of lanes and alleyways where the houses were crowded so close together, their jetties almost touched. I kept to the kennel and picked my way carefully through the filth. Church bells, which were always rung to mark a death, now tolled continually. Fires were lit at every sixth house and kept burning day and night in the vain hope they would keep the plague at bay. The smoke caught in my eyes and made them sting and water. Black smuts and grey flakes of ash swirled in the air. I could hardly tell where I was or see where I was going.

I stumbled along Carter Lane, then passed under the shadow of St Paul's, quite empty now of people, until I reached the City wall and the Ludgate. There I was stopped by a guard who told me that I needed a bill of health, signed by a constable and certifying that I was free from the plague. Without it he would not let me pass through. I pleaded. I begged. I grew angry. To no avail. I was turned back.

When I reached home, I found my father was dead. He lay where he had fallen down, on the parlour floor. My mother had not even covered his body with a sheet. It seemed that the shock of his death had made her take leave of her wits. For though she had been forever scolding and chastising him, I do believe that in her heart she did truly care for him. Just as I did.

While my mother ran hither and thither about the house, looking for any valuables my father might have hidden away, I fetched a sheet from the linen chest. As my mother, calling and talking out loud to herself the whole while, turned out cupboards, scrabbled under beds and pulled up loose floorboards, I knelt down beside his still-warm body and rested my head against his chest. Hot tears coursed down my cheeks and soaked his shirt. Then, when I had said a prayer and bid him a last farewell, I covered his body with the sheet and went to comfort my mother.

I found her in the kitchen, her clothes all disordered

and her eyes wild and dark. The minute she saw me, she pulled out her pocket from under her skirts and emptied it out on to the table.

"See, Margrat. All we have in the world is this!" She scooped up the three half crowns in her hands and held them out to me. "What will happen to us now your father is gone?"

We clung silently to each other in the gathering darkness. The guttering flame of our last candle flickered and went out, as two black rats swarmed up the candlestick and started to eat the candle. The horror of it. It was the longest and most terrible night of my life. All I could hear was the endless tolling of the bells, the scratching, scrabbling, squealing of rats as they took over the house... and my mother's wracking sobs. When it was over and the smoke-grey light of early morning began to filter through the shutters, I knew I could no longer be the child. For I had no doting father to take care of me. And my mother, who, though she had many faults, had always seemed so strong and capable, now clung desperately to me.

So, when there came a loud knocking at the door, it was a quite different Margrat who answered. One who was unwashed, bedraggled and exhausted to the very core of her soul.

If I had opened the door to the Devil himself, I would have fallen into his arms, so grateful was I to see another living being. How much better that it was Nicholas come to see how we fared. And on hearing that my father was dead and my mother losing her wits, he stepped in at once, closing the door quickly behind him. Then, his hands resting lightly on my shoulders, he looked down at me, saying, "No one must know that your father has died, Margrat, or the searchers will come and the house will be sealed up. No, there is nothing else for it, but I must bury his body in the cellar. Whilst I do that, you must attend to your mother. Get her to bed. Make her comfortable. Fetch water and wash her face. Then you must give her some of this…"

He gave me another of his brown glass bottles full of a clear liquid this time. "Three drops only, on the tongue."

I nodded, slipped the bottle into my pocket and turned from him and went as if to find my mother. But the minute he had disappeared into the parlour, I crept after him. I had this overwhelming need to see my father one last time.

I watched from behind the door, as Nicholas knelt down beside him and pulled back the sheet. I saw that he checked under my father's shirt for swellings. He sighed as if greatly relieved and it was then that I heard him say, "I am sorry for your death John. And for Catherine's. Truly I am. But it had to be done, for what are two deaths now when soon all may be raised from the dead?"

Then he bent down to gather up my father's body. I thought he would not lift it, but in his last days, my father had shrunk to skin and bone and was as light as a baby's breath. I ran quickly up into the shadow of the stairs, peering down as I watched him carry my father down into the cellar.

Very soon, out through the cellar door rose the sour, musty smell of damp, freshly dug earth. I could not bear to think on what was happening there and so hurried up the stairs to find some consolation in helping my mother.

I found her kneeling beside her bed, her face pressed into the folds of my father's nightshirt. I reached out and stroked her hair... something I would never have dared to do before, my mother hating any outward displays of affection. Now she grabbed my hand, pulled me down till my face was level with hers and smothered it with frantic kisses.

"Come," I said, trying to gentle my voice. The smoke

and little sleep had made it sound rough and harsh. I helped her undress down to her shift and lifted her up into bed. Then I poured water out from the ewer into the basin and dampening a cloth, wiped her face. "Now, Nicholas says I must give you this," I pulled out the glass bottle and held it up.

At the mention of his name, a ghost of a smile and she dutifully opened her mouth. I counted out the drops. Only three. Then I sat by the bed and rested my cheek against her hand, like a mother comforting a sick child. Worn out, we both fell into a deep sleep.

◦둏 ⓖ◦

When I awoke it was night again. All the candles were lit and burned bright. My mother had turned away from me, but was still fast asleep.

We were not alone. Nicholas sat quietly in a chair by the door. His eyes were closed. His hands, fingers laced, rested on his thighs. His dark hair fell loose around his shoulders. His breathing was deep, hypnotic almost. His waistcoat was unbuttoned. The strings of his white linen shirt were undone. Streaks of earth from the cellar floor had dried light brown on the black of his breeches and soiled the ruffled ribbons. Even in candlelight, I could see his russet shoes were now quite ruined.

The heat of the room was stifling. I could feel the sweat trickle between my breasts. I struggled to breathe. It was as if the walls of the room were closing in and would squeeze the life out of me. I could think of nothing but my father. See nothing but his face disappearing as Nicholas covered it with earth. It felt as if I was being buried too. From the street I heard the creak and rumble of cart wheels and the watchman crying, "Bring out your dead". It was then I started to scream. I ran to the window and struggled to open it, my hands scrabbling frantically against the yellowing diamonds of glass.

Within moments, Nicholas was up from his chair and his arms were tight about me and I was rocked as gently as if I was a baby. "Margrat, Margrat," he whispered into my hair, "Ssshh. Come away. Your father is dead. Calling for the watchman will not bring him back. Listen to me. You are tired and hungry and must let me take care of you now."

I felt so very weary. My limbs felt heavy. My speech came out dull and slurred. I struggled to keep my eyes open. I thought, if only I could just lie down and sleep, when I awoke I would surely find it had just been another bad dream. And when morning came, things did at first seem a little better. Nicholas was gone and my mother was awake and dressed. The fire in the kitchen was lit. She had fetched fresh water from the well. There was fresh bread on the table. And apart from an aching head, she seemed almost herself again, though gentler still, for she smiled at me, saying, "The Doctor had business to attend to. He went out before first light. Now I must go and see to the shop. But you must stay here, Margrat. The Doctor made me swear on my life that you would. I will not be gone long."

But I could not bear to be left alone in the house with my father's body. So I stood on the step and watched as she turned the corner into Carter Lane.

Pulling the door shut behind me, I followed her. Close enough to keep her in sight, but not so close that she might turn and see me.

She was passing through St Paul's churchyard, just as the cathedral bells began to ring out. She stopped and looked up at the great bell tower, as if she was waiting to see what hour it was. Then, just as if she had been felled by a musket shot, I saw her hands fly up to her chest and she crumpled and fell down. By the time that I reached her, she was struggling for breath. Her fingers and lips were turning blue.

We were not far from home, but I could not lift or carry her on my own. And though people passed by and

I cried out to them for help, fearing the plague, they covered their noses and mouths and hurried on.

I grew desperate. I ran about crying, "Pity. For God's sake take pity on us."

I was so distracted that I did not see that my prayer had been answered. Now there was someone at my mother's side. He was bent down over her. What was it that he did?

In horror I saw who it was. I ran at him, raining a shower of blows down on his back with my fists. "Leave her alone. Leave her alone. Get away from her." But he took no notice and lifted her up and started to walk away. I ran alongside him, grabbing at the tatters of his shirt in an effort to make him stop. My mother's head lolled against his chest and she hung limp as a rag doll in his arms. By the time we were at the end of Carter Lane and I saw that he was carrying her home, his pale gold hair had turned dark with sweat and his strength had nearly ebbed away. "Presque là." he gasped, staggering on.

"I thought you had left London." I was struggling to keep up. "Now you risk everything to help me. Why, when I would not accept what you had told me?"

He said nothing. He did not need to. I believed he had done it to gain my trust.

I looked at him, his arms trembling under the strain of bearing my mother's weight. He was thin and filthy from living, God knows how, on the streets.

I felt a spark of pity for him. He did not look in the least wicked or evil. I did not think he meant to abduct me or had the strength to do so. I reached out and touched his hand and for one brief moment, a spark of common humanity connected us. Then all was pandemonium and Nicholas was upon us, come out of nowhere.

I cannot be sure what happened then, but I saw Nicholas snatch at Christophe's arm. As Christophe tried to shake himself free, my mother slid from his grasp and tumbled to the ground. There was the glint of a steel blade and Nicholas sprang back, clutching his arm. Blood seeped through his fingers. A knife fell to the ground between them and in that brief second, as Nicholas bent to pick it up, Christophe touched my hand and looked beseechingly at me. Then he turned and fled.

Nicholas, triumphant, took off his coat and, rolling up his shirtsleeve, showed me the knife wound. "It does not run deep. But see how dangerous he is, Margrat."

Now I was confused, for I recognised the knife.

My father had used it for cutting papers. I had seen it only days before, on his desk. It was not Christophe's knife. Hunched down in the dirt and cradling my mother's head in my lap, I was forced to consider what this might mean. Nicholas had cut himself... *and with my father's knife.*

Chapter 8

The next morning as she staggered into the kitchen, still half asleep, Claire was met with an angry "I suppose you're going to say you forgot?" There was her mum, standing, back to the sink, glaring at her.

"What? Forgot what?"

"That Robert called."

"Oh." She'd known that he *would* call. No point in pretending she'd forgotten. Better brazen it out. Go on the attack. "Mum, he's a creep. A weirdo."

"Don't be so silly," her mum snapped, pulling on rubber gloves and turning to start on the washing up. "He's a well-respected antiques dealer. I'm not as stupid as you think, you know. I've checked him out. He is who he says he is." Claire could see her mum's shoulders tense up. There was a moment's silence and then a rush of words, "He rang this morning, as it happens."

"And?"

"And I told him we'd love to go for tea on Thursday."

The day before her birthday, as if that made any difference to anything. But she'd promised herself she'd be kinder to her mum, more understanding, so she tried again. "Mum, listen. Please. There's something not right about him. He wears weird clothes. He talks funny. He freaks..." But she never got to finish the sentence.

"We're going and that's that. He wants to buy that box. And he's willing to pay shed loads of money for it." And there was a dangerous edge to her mum's voice, which Claire knew she shouldn't ignore.

"I'm not going and I'm not going to let you sell the box either." Claire twisted the ring round her finger. Round and round and round.

Her mum turned, a wine glass full of soap bubbles in one hand. "Don't you dare tell me..." Anger made her squeeze the glass tight. Thin and delicate, it shattered into a cascade of tiny pieces; the noise of it, clear and bright, shocking them into silence.

They both looked down at the splinters of glass scattered everywhere.

"Oh damn," her mum said. Then they both started to giggle. "That was Grandma's favourite glass." She was starting to peel off her rubber gloves, when Claire saw all the colour drain out of her face.

"Mum?"

An almost imperceptible shake of the head as the gloves fell to the floor and, whoosh, she was gone. Claire could hear footsteps pounding up the stairs and then a door slamming.

For a split-second Claire stood there, her stomach clenching into a knot at this latest inexplicable twist on the emotional roller coaster they were all riding now. She sighed, got out the dustpan and brush from the cupboard under the sink and started to sweep up the glass. But then she heard a horrible groaning, retching sound coming from upstairs. The sound of someone being sick.

Claire dropped the brush and ran. "Mum, MUM!" She pushed open the bathroom door and looked down at her mum, kneeling with her head over the toilet bowl. "Are you okay?" Claire knelt down beside her. Her mum reached back and fumbled for Claire's hand and gave it a squeeze. Later, when she'd stopped vomiting and looking like death, she'd said, "It was just something I ate, that's all."

But Claire thought she still seemed worried and distracted and not as full of life as she had been. *Maybe it's the heat,* she thought. It was sapping the life out of all of them. It hung like a pall over the city, making everything shimmer and blur. There was no relief from the soaring temperature… not even early in the morning or late at night. Claire couldn't sleep and she felt tired all the time. Even Micky had black circles under her eyes and lolled around as if all her bones had turned to liquid jelly. Claire didn't even have the energy to argue about the visit. Or say 'no' when her mum said Robert would be coming to pick them up; save them from travelling on the underground in all that heat. She'd be 14 in a few days' time, but it still seemed that she had no control over anything about her life. Not even the little things.

I have to get out, she thought. There'd been talk on the television about banning events where lots of people would be crowded in together. But it hadn't happened yet and the circus was on tomorrow and she would go and not tell her mum.

Well, she was nearly 14. So she said she was going to see Jade, which was, strictly speaking, the truth. And she asked if Jade could come back and sleep over. That way she wouldn't have to travel home late at night, on her own. Then she sent Jade a text and arranged a time to meet outside the circus.

The circus was in Jubilee Gardens on the Embankment. She'd been there before with her mum, dad and Micky for the Festival of the Thames. So she knew exactly where she was going and as soon as she was out of the tube and in sight of the gardens, she could see the circus tent. It was massive. Red-and-white striped, like a giant piece of sugar candy.

She was standing around outside, feeling hot and sticky, waiting for Jade and idly reading the blurb about the forthcoming circus stunt that would see two young French wire-walkers cross the Thames on a wire strung 45 metres above the river. Then her phone rang. "Oh, no! Okay. Yeah, I know you're sorry. Hope it's not flu. Hope she feels better soon." It was Jade, saying her mum had rung her to say she felt suddenly ill and needed Jade to turn round and go straight home to look after her baby brother. That meant Claire would have to go in on her own, or go home, too. And she definitely *wasn't* going to do that.

Inside the circus tent it was stiflingly hot and airless. There was the smell of trodden, bruised grass. Acrid fumes, making her eyes sting, drifting in from the generators outside. And something else, something comforting and familiar, a sharp chalky sourness, a sweaty trainer smell that made her think of school.

Tiers of wooden benches rose up around the circus ring, which was empty except for three jugglers practising with lit torches. She could hear the swish and faint roar of the flame as they whirled them through the air. See the traces of light left behind like a phosphorescence.

Something caught her eye. She looked up. High on a wire, a figure in a white singlet and dark sweatpants was carefully, meticulously, practising somersaults. Like a wheel turning. Slowly. Slowly. There was no safety net. Claire frowned. Something seemed familiar. What? Then she remembered. The boy in her dream, dancing on the wire and beckoning to her. A feeling as she watched, mesmerised, willing the figure to stay safe, that another piece of the puzzle was about to fall into place.

"Hey!"

Claire snapped round. A young woman… 19, maybe 20, but smaller even than Claire, and with a halo of red-gold hair, (and a perfectly straight nose. How annoying was that!) was placing a hand on Claire's shoulder. "What are you doing?"

Flustered, Claire bent down and hurriedly scrabbled in her backpack for the tickets. Held one out to the young woman, who said, sharply, "You are early. We are not starting yet. *Rentrez plus tard.*"

Come back later. She would have snatched the ticket out of Claire's right hand, but Claire held on to it tightly and could feel the tension rising. Could see the tendons in the young woman's neck stand out and her jaw clench in irritation. Her grey eyes turning dark and two high spots of colour appearing suddenly on her cheeks. Claire registered her single earring, a tiny gold 'ankh'… the Egyptian symbol of life.

Then in a flash she was all smiles, "But that's okay. It's good you are here. People are not coming because of the flu. You can stay and watch if you like. *Pas de problème*. My name is Jacalyn by the way. Oh and I love your ring. Where did you get it?" Her voice suddenly light and bubbling. Happy.

Claire instinctively covered the ring with her other hand. There was a second's pause and then when Claire didn't answer the question, Jacalyn, tilting her head in the direction of the high wire, said, " Okay. I'm going up. Of course I am not as *casse-cou*, as dare-devil as my twin brother Zacharie. Now he is something else..." And an expression, a startling mixture of love but also contempt, flickered across Jacalyn's face. "But I promise you would be safe with me!"

Claire must have looked horrified, because the young woman laughed and said, "It's okay. I am joking. Only Zacharie would risk taking a complete novice up on the wire. You can just watch from down here!"

So Claire did. Saw Jacalyn clamber swiftly up. Saw Zacharie stop, then walk effortlessly along the wire towards his sister, exchange words and touch hands in passing. And as Zacharie took a first step on the ladder, he turned his head and looked straight at Claire. A shiver ran up her spine and she felt her pulse racing.

She watched him climbing down, until she was distracted by a troupe of tumblers who'd appeared in the ring and had started somersaulting and leaping over each other.

Quickly they formed a trembling pyramid of bodies, three tumblers at the bottom, then two and one at the very top who caught her eye. Once he knew she was watching, the top tumbler started to wobble exaggeratedly, pretending he was going to fall, all the while blowing her kisses and making rude gestures with his hands.

And then the other tumblers were shouting angrily, telling him to stop. But it was too late, because the pyramid was tottering and swaying wildly and the tumblers were staggering towards her. She knew with absolute certainty what would happen. The pyramid would collapse, crushing her. *"Schoolgirl, 14, takes fatal tumble with six acrobats!"* She would have smiled, but her lips, her feet, her brain, her *whole body* seemed totally frozen.

But she did hear the shout. *"Imbéciles! Idiots!"* Felt an arm around her shoulders. Registered a warm, musky smell, as she was scooped out of the way of the collapsing pyramid.

"*Merde!*"

Then a face, close to hers, its hair, the same pale gold as Jacalyn's, but fine and straight, brushing her cheek. Its grey eyes wide with concern. Its beautifully shaped mouth that made her want to reach up and trace its outline with her finger. Now the mouth was smiling and she could see the teeth, small and white like a child's, making the face look oddly vulnerable. Though it was not at all the face of a little boy. And the white singlet he wore showed the clear definition of every muscle.

This was the closest she'd ever been to someone quite so beautiful and it was making her feel light-headed.

"Oh… okay. You need to sit down. *Vite!*"

He steered her towards the first tier of seats and sat with her, his arm heavy around her shoulders. Claire pressed a hand against her mouth. All of a sudden, she felt horribly sick. Looked up at him. "Sorry. Sorry. It must be the shock."

"No problem." And he tucked her hair back behind her ear, his touch unexpectedly soft and gentle. And it was then that she noticed it. On the third finger of his right hand. A ring. An exact copy of hers. She held her hand out towards him, fingers splayed. "It's the same ring. Yours and mine." She felt a flutter of excitement in her throat.

"Oh, *mon dieu*! You are right! That is so bizarre." (Pronouncing it bee-zarrr. Cute!) "And I have never seen one like it ever before, have you?"

She shook her head. "Where did you get yours?" Maybe he'd be able to tell her something about it. Where it came from.

"It was my father's. But he died when I was just a little boy."

"Oh," Claire's hand reached out and touched his, "I didn't mean…"

"That's okay. And it was my mother who gave me the ring, told me I must wear it. I said, '*Non!*' I really didn't want to. I felt like a freak… a small boy wearing a ring, it is, you know…"

"Bee-zarr…" Claire couldn't help herself. It just popped out. Shit. But he seemed to think it was funny.

"Yes. Bee-zarr! And I got teased a lot about the ring, too. My twin sister, Jacalyn, said she would wear it instead. But my mother said that it had to be me, because I was a boy. That made Jacalyn so cross. She said that was rubbish… that of course a girl could wear it too and besides, I was too irresponsible, too wild and worse even than that… I didn't believe the *histoire*, the stories about a prophecy and our family being guardians of a great secret. Jacalyn of course believes every word of it. Circus people… so superstitious. But it is weird though, because however much I grow, the ring still fits my finger. That is amazing. Like magic! Oh and sorry. I talk too much. I have a big mouth."

But beautiful. Very, very beautiful!

"What about you?" His eyes held hers and his hand, broad and hard and strong, reached across and touched her cheek, just long enough to send a shock wave running through her, making her catch her breath. "Where did you get your ring? Maybe someone in your family ran away to join the circus?"

"I wish!"

"You wouldn't like it… believe me." His face looked suddenly troubled. Serious. "Up on the high wire. The excitement. The adrenaline rush. All that is brilliant. I love it. But the circus *family*. Pah! So many people knowing everything about you. No room to breathe. No escape. My sister always *there*… always messing in my life as if being my twin gives her the right. I would do *anything* to get away…" But then he was suddenly smiling again, saying, "Sorry. Didn't mean to say all that… but somehow I feel I can tell you anything. Maybe the rings bind us together! Maybe we have… how do you say… telepathic communication? Let me see." He closed his eyes and frowned… pretending to read her mind. "Your mad, bad great uncle left the ring to you in his will… on condition you wire-walk across Niagara Falls… Don't worry, I can teach you!"

"No! Silly. My grandma died and left it to me. And when I put it on it fitted perfectly! Just like yours. And mine won't come off either. I've tried everything. Look!" Claire was pulling and pulling at the ring.

"*Je sais*. I tried too. Believe me. I'd give Jacalyn the ring just to shut her up! But now I've met you, well I am beginning to wonder, are the stories true?" He looked as if he meant every word of what he was saying and Claire felt a great wave of relief and excitement break over her. She wasn't going mad. Zacharie's ring behaved in the same way as hers. And now there was someone she could talk to about it who *wouldn't* think she was insane.

Chapter 8

But there was not time, not yet anyway, because the circus tent was suddenly full of people and noise as a group of Italian students flooded in.

"Zacharie!" An older man with long grey hair tied back in a ponytail was calling him.

Zacharie turned. "*Merde!* You see what I mean... no escape! I'll have to go. Are you coming to join the workshop? Please say you will. I'll look after you. Promise!"

"No. No thanks." She didn't want him to see how hopeless she was. That she had no sense of balance and couldn't even catch a ball when it was thrown to her from a metre away.

"Have you got a pen then?"

Claire nodded and rummaged in her backpack. Then Zacharie took her hand, turned it over and wrote his mobile phone number on the inside of her wrist.

"In case I don't see you later. It is always manic after the show and I might not. Oh and my name is Zacharie... but you can call me Zac if you want. Call me? *Tu promis?* Oh and *your* name, I don't know it."

"Claire." She nodded. "And I promise."

She watched as he ran off. She couldn't stop

herself. He moved so beautifully and with such confidence. Then he was swallowed up by the group of students. She looked down at the number on her wrist. Touched it with her little finger. It smudged. She looked in her backpack for her notebook and copied the number down carefully on the inside of the back cover. And then tore out a piece of paper and wrote the number on that too, folded it and pushed it far down in her jeans pocket. Insurance!

Claire stayed and watched the workshop. Felt her heart miss a beat as Zacharie turned and looked in her direction. She'd had to look away quickly and pretend she wasn't watching him. But she was, especially when he was helping a slim and beautiful girl turn cartwheels. Placing his hands on her hips and guiding her round.

That could have been me, she thought, if only I'd been braver.

* * *

The show was awesome. Especially Zacharie. Jacalyn was right, he was totally fearless and Claire found it hard to watch as he danced on the wire. And there was an excitement in knowing that she 'knew' him. That she'd felt his arm around her. Her fingers went up, instinctively, to tuck her hair behind her ears, touch where he had touched. And she had his mobile number. And he'd made her promise to call him! Mmm. She'd been going to leave early, get home before it got too dark. But the temptation to wait, see him again after the show, won out against her fear of being alone at night, on the tube. So she waited. Waited until the last seat in the big top was empty. Sat on for a while, watching as the ring was cleared. But there was no sign of Zacharie or Jacalyn anywhere. Several texts from her mum though. She looked at her watch. Ten o'clock. Texted back, '*On my way.*' She'd have to go now.

But as she went out, Jacalyn was standing by the entrance.

"Hey again! Did you enjoy it? And Zac? He's amazing, *hein?*" She was smiling… a look of wry amusement at Claire's expression. "Yeah! All the girls chase him. But he never gets caught. A real, how do you say… breaker of hearts."

"It was great!" Claire was shifting from foot to

foot, feeling awkward and wanting to escape now. "But I have to go… get back home. I hate…"

"Wait!" And Zacharie was there beside her, dressed now in black jeans and a white T-shirt. Smiling. Looking really pleased to see her… reaching out to touch her arm with a finger. Making her shiver.

But Jacalyn didn't look pleased at all. She looked cross. "For God's sake, Zac… she's way too young for you. Leave her alone." Claire felt herself tensing up. Being treated like a child again. It made her so angry. But if Jacalyn thought Zac would react, she was disappointed. He just stood with his arms crossed, smiling. Jacalyn hovered around for a second, unsure what to do. Then she stormed off. Zacharie made a face at Claire. "She is *reloue*. You know, a pain in the – how do you say? – butt."

She couldn't stop herself looking down and thinking how perfect *his* was and felt herself going hot all over. And *how childish was that?* "I've got to go," she said quickly. "If I'm late home…"

"I'll come with you. Keep you safe! Where do you live? And then we can talk about the rings! Wait… I'll just get my jacket." And he sped off towards a huddle of trailers tucked behind the Big Top.

And Claire was still standing there, feeling happy that at last something *nice* was happening, when Jacalyn came back. She was smiling, so Claire was caught off guard when she spat out the words. "A warning. Stay away from him. He plays around. You don't need the complication. You can sort it without him you know. Go on. Go home…"

Claire was shocked. Flustered. What did she mean… *sort it without him*. Sort what? Maybe she should ask? But Jacalyn stood there, implacable… her arms folded tight across her body. Intimidating. Scary. There was no sign of Zacharie.

Claire ran.

She was used to travelling on the tube, but not at night and on her own. So she felt anxious and she was still upset and angry at what Jacalyn had said. How it had made her feel silly, childish, humiliated, confused. "Stupid cow. She's just jealous, that's all. She can go screw herself!"

But it wasn't really that late and in spite of the flu, there were plenty of people around. Too many. The tube was packed, though everyone was trying to create little exclusion zones around themselves and looked horrified when anyone sneezed or coughed. A few people were wearing masks and there were no babies in buggies, no small children. Claire had to straphang, her backpack tucked between her feet because there was nowhere to sit. It was stiflingly hot. She could hardly breathe. So when the train stopped and people got out, she made a beeline for an empty seat and sat down gratefully, hugging her backpack close. But then, as she took a deep breath in relief, something, and she didn't know what it was at first, started to make her feel uneasy. She scanned the carriage hurriedly. Just the usual mix of people. Nothing alarming. Except the smell. The perfume. She'd been so busy thinking of Zacharie, that for a while she'd forgotten about *HIM*. She breathed in slowly, tasted the air. Yes, there it was. Cinnamon and flowers. Faint but insistent. She looked around anxiously, but the carriage was full and there were too many people standing for her to be able to see to the end.

He could be here, she thought. *Why not?* A coincidence. Her mum had met an old boyfriend like that once. "The carriage doors opened," she'd said, "and there he was, getting out as I was getting in. And I hadn't seen him for 15 years! Amazing."

And it had to be a¯ coincidence, didn't it? Because the alternative was unthinkable.

She thought she would walk up the hill from the tube station, then along the side of the common and into Grandma's road. But as she came out of the tube station, she felt as if she was being followed. When she turned, out of the corner of her eye, she caught a flicker of something, someone turning away as if to hide from her. So, when she saw the bus coming, she didn't think twice, darted across the road and as soon as the doors opened, she leaped on, pushing past a whole queue of people. But she didn't care. She just wanted to be somewhere light and full of people. Somewhere she'd feel safe.

She passed her travel card across the sensor, then dropped down sideways into a seat right at the front of the bus, her legs sticking into the aisle and her eyes fixed on the door of the bus. That way she could see everyone who got on. And even after the doors had closed and the bus had pulled away, she still kept looking. Expecting any moment he'd pop up, or she'd smell the cinnamon and flowers.

But it was only a few stops and, when she got off the bus, she ran fast all the way to Grandma's house. Didn't stop to look back and see if anyone was there. Just ran. Then she panicked when she couldn't find her key and banged on the door like someone demented and rang the bell and clattered the letter box.

"What on earth?" her mum stepped back hurriedly from the doorway as Claire cannoned through, slammed the door behind her and leaned against it, breathing hard.

Claire's mum went to push her aside and open the door. "What on earth's the matter? Where's Jade?"

"Jade's not here. Her mum was feeling poorly so Jade stayed with her." Not really a lie at all.

"Oh. So you came home all on your own?"

"It was fine. It was okay."

"Then why were you running? What's happened?"

"Nothing. Honest. I just thought I saw... heard someone behind me. That's all... and I got scared. Stupid. There wasn't anyone."

"Hmm." Claire's mum opened her mouth to

say something and then thought better of it. "Well you're all right and that's the main thing. But I hope Jade's mum is feeling better. God, I hope it's not flu. Do you think…"

"Mum! I'm going to bed okay? I'm really tired…"

Claire was lying on the bed, in the dark, fully clothed. She wanted to be quiet and still so she could think about things. About him, Robert. Had Robert been following her? She was sure he had. About Grandma leaving tickets for a circus where the wire-walker had a ring just like hers. About Zacharie.

She scrabbled upright in bed, reached over and picked up her phone from the bedside table. Then she lay back down again, holding the phone to her chest. Maybe she could just send him a text. Just a '*Hi!*' and a smiley face. There wouldn't be any harm in that, would there? He'd wonder where she'd disappeared to. And so what if the things Jacalyn had said about him were true… he was only ever going to be a friend, wasn't he? Someone who'd understand about the ring. Nothing more. And if he wanted to reply he could, because then he'd have her number. And if he didn't…

She lay a long while thinking about it… building up the courage to do it. Heard her mum coming up the stairs and hurriedly pulled the covers over and pretended to be asleep. Then, when she heard her mum's bedroom door close, she pulled out the piece of paper from her jeans pocket and unfolded it. She could just read the number in the light from her phone. She keyed it in, saved it to memory and then wrote the text, took a deep breath, and sent it.

And waited and then fell asleep and it was gone two o'clock when the message came in. Click. *'I thought I'd lost you! Now I can sleep! Zxx'*

* * *

Robert's house, tucked away behind the Strand just over the river from the Jubilee Gardens, was spectacular. Even Claire could see that and took a surreptitious picture of it on her phone. It looked really old and was made of worn red brick and weathered stone. It had tall glittering windows and, between them, plaster panels decorated with Egyptian figures in relief. Steps led up to a great carved wooden door and into a panelled hall large enough to take the biggest fireplace Claire had ever seen.

It was a pity there wasn't a fire lit, Claire thought, because even though the heat outside was like a furnace, the cold from the stone floor still struck up through the soles of her shoes.

She didn't like it here. She knew he could see that. Because, although he was paying a lot of attention to her mum and Micky, he was watching her. She could feel it. And she knew absolutely that he HAD been following her too. She'd thought about refusing to come today, but wanted to see where he lived. It was important somehow. And anyway, she wasn't about to let her mum and Micky go off with him alone.

"Let me show you around," he said and her mum was saying, "Oh, yes please," and following after him with the biggest smile on her face, as if he were offering to show her the crown jewels, then let her try them on.

Even Micky was excited by the tapestry hanging over the chimney piece in the room he called 'the great parlour'. A man in armour thrusting his sword up into the belly of a huge, fire-breathing dragon.

Then while Claire's mum went to the loo – she said she was feeling queasy with the heat – he showed them the library with its illuminated medieval manuscripts, as bright as jewels, laid out in glass cases. And in the corner of the room, standing in shadow, was a decorated wooden mummy case painted with the life-size image of a woman. She was dark-eyed and full-lipped and had two ropes of black hair framing her face. Micky spotted it at once, ran over, "Can I touch it?" Her hand reached out; hovered over the case.

"You can look inside if you like."

"Oh!"

He lifted the lid off and to one side.

"That is wicked!" Micky said, turning to Claire and reaching back to tug at her hand. "Look!"

Claire reluctantly peered in. The mummy had been half unwrapped. *Poor thing,* she thought, with her sunken eyes and stretched yellow skin and horrible tufts of dull red hair... and the third finger of her right hand missing.

"Does she have a name?" Micky asked.

"She does," Robert said, pointing to a cartouche on the mummy's case. "Nefertaru, priestess and dancer at the temple of the Lady of Red Linen, the Bringer of Plagues, the goddess Sekhmet."

"Sekhmet?" Claire looked startled. There it was again. That name.

"How cool is that?" breathed Micky, eyes wide and round as saucers. "And look!" Micky had noticed the missing finger too. "I bet she had a ring, just like Claire's, that wouldn't come off, and somebody chopped off her finger to get it." Micky was looking enquiringly at Robert.

"Mmm." He looked thoughtful. "It is said that only death can part the wearer from the ring...and it's said to protect the wearer from sickness too... so maybe she was *murdered* for it. What do you think?"

He's teasing, Claire thought. *Isn't he?*

He was pointing to some other hicroglyphs. "She was only just 14 when she died."

"Eugh... Claire... just like you," Micky started to say. "Now you're going to have to wear the ring always, unless..."

But then Claire's mum came back into the room.

God, Claire thought, distracted for a split-second from what Micky was saying, *you do look awful, even though you've brushed your hair and put on lipgloss.*

"What's that about Claire's ring?" her mum said, trying to sound upbeat and cheerful, "And who had their finger chopped off?"

Micky told her.

"Oh, so does that make Claire Sekhmet's priestess too, then? And does the ring protect her from ALL sorts of plague?" Her mum was joking, had started to laugh, but looking from Claire's face to Robert's, she stopped, taken aback to see how neither of them was smiling. She tried to lighten things up by saying and half meaning it, "So Claire's okay, but what about me? What about Micky? What's going to protect US from this bird flu? We haven't got any fancy rings."

It was then that he'd taken them up to his study, with its shelves of boxes and bottles and books. And as they climbed up the stairs, Claire trailing reluctantly behind, he talked about the clear tincture, the 'medicine' he made up himself, "Just three drops, every day, straight onto the tongue. It's perfectly safe… So safe, even pregnant women can take it." Robert reached out and touched her mum on the arm. The briefest of contact, but it made Claire want to knock his hand away and shout *Don't touch her!* "And you'll be protected against every kind of plague. It's always worked for me. Because really you know I'm over four hundred years old!"

Micky and her mum laughed and her mum said, "You look amazing for four hundred. You haven't got a magic cream have you? Only I'd kill for some of that."

"Who wouldn't? No, just the medicine. I'll give you some to take home..."

Claire could see her mum was going to be sucked right in by it. She had a dressing table overflowing with pills and potions.

When Robert opened his study door, Claire's mum and Micky went straight in. Claire meant to follow on, but the smell hit her... whoomph... and stopped her dead in her tracks. Cinnamon and flowers. Her mum and Micky didn't even notice it or see her reaction. But he did. Their eyes locked.

He held out his hand to her. "Come in," he said, his fingers lacing through hers and pulling her towards him.

"No!"

Claire's mum turned, smiling. "What's the matter?" But Claire couldn't answer, because she didn't know. Couldn't say why a smell should fill her with such fear.

She pulled her hand free and turned and ran and didn't stop running until she was out of the house and had slammed the door behind her. Now she was in the open air, she felt better, though the smell still clung to her. She dropped down onto the top step and sat there, her heart racing. And when the door opened behind her, for a minute she was terrified it was him.

"What on earth's got into you?" Her mum sounded concerned, but exasperated and bewildered too. "You silly girl," she said, bending down, enveloping Claire in a curtain of hair, the smell, THAT smell clinging to her and intense in the heat. "Robert wants you to come back inside. He's worried he's upset you... all that stupid joking about the ring." Her hand rested on Claire's shoulder, rubbing it as if she was a child again and needing to be soothed.

Claire shook her head and felt tears prickle at the back of her nose.

"Well stay here then." Her mum's voice

sounded flat and tired. "You know where we are."

But there was no way Claire was going back inside. She would stay out here, move along the step until she was in the shade, rest her back against the warm brick of the house and wait.

* * *

When they came out of the house at last, the heat was still suffocating but had lost some of its fierceness. The noise of traffic had reached a deafening crescendo. It was rush hour and people were on the move. Masses more people in cars now. Safe, isolated, cocooned from everyone else.

The drive home took a long time and there was hardly a word spoken the whole journey. Robert had insisted on driving them back home too. "Too risky for your mum to be travelling on the tube in her condition," he'd said, looking at Claire and smiling conspiratorially, as if they shared a secret.

Micky was asleep on the back seat, her mouth open and her head lolling against Claire's shoulder, making it damp with sweat and dribble. In one hand she was clutching a little figure which *he* had given her as a parting present; a genuine

Ancient Egyptian magical figurine (he'd said): a wax doll, with a fragment of papyrus inserted in its back, strands of dull red hair pushed into its head. He'd explained there was a spell written on the papyrus, which would protect the bearer from harm. He'd given Claire's mum one too, which she'd popped in her bag for safe keeping. Nothing for Claire though. He'd said she didn't need it. She had the ring. And it was then that she'd done something really stupid. Had blurted out, "*One* of the rings!" And he had taken her arm and tucked it in his and leaned in and whispered, "Ah, yes… the little rope-walker at the Cirque du Sekhmet."

So he *had* followed her.

Claire's mum sat in the front passenger seat, her hands folded in her lap and with her head turned to look out of the window.

He seemed to be concentrating on the traffic now, but when Claire glanced up, their eyes met in the rear-view mirror and in that second, panic rose up in her so fast she struggled to control it. She felt he sensed that and was pleased by it.

Breathe, she thought. *Deep breaths and steady your thoughts. Don't let him win.*

Then he half turned towards her mum and said something, in a low voice that Claire couldn't catch. But it made her mum laugh and that startled Claire. She should have been pleased her mum was happy, but she wasn't. Not one little bit. And she was even less pleased when they got home and Robert helped her mum out of the car and then opened the back door and went to lift Micky out *as if he was part of their family*. She was still fast asleep. Claire moved roughly, deliberately, letting Micky's head fall awkwardly from her shoulder, hoping it would wake her up. "Thanks. I don't need your help. I can manage."

And it must have been while Claire was busy getting Micky out of the car and inside and onto the sofa, that her mum had fetched it for him. Sold it.

Once the front door was closed and they could hear his car pulling away, her mum had exploded. "The man you've been so spectacularly rude to all afternoon has just paid an enormous sum of money for your Grandma's old box. I *told* you he would. Look!" She pulled out a huge wodge of money from her handbag and waved it under Claire's nose.

Not an enormous sum of money, she thought.

He would have paid more. "How could you?" Anger welling up inside Claire and spilling out. "Wait till I tell Dad what you've done. It was MY box."

Claire's mum quietly tucked the money back in her bag. "We need the money... and that's that."

"You're a stupid cow. No wonder Dad left you." Tears were streaming down Claire's face now. She turned on her heel, ran upstairs, went straight into Grandma's bedroom, saw the empty space on the chair where the box ought to have been and threw herself down on the bed.

It was still happening. Things being done to her and she had no control over any of it. But she could *take* control. She could. Robert might have the box now, but as far as she knew, he still had no way of unlocking it. He still needed her for that. She was sure of it. Or Zacharie. Maybe his ring? She sat up and wiped away the tears with the back of her hand. She had to talk to Zac. Warn him. She looked at her watch. He wouldn't answer. There was the evening performance at the circus and he would be high up on the wire. That was okay. She'd leave a voice message. "Don't think I'm mad, but there's this man who knows about our rings. He scares me. And there's a box, a very special box my grandma left me and the ring is the key. Only it won't open it. Not yet. And now *he* has the box. And he followed me to the circus. And he knows about you. And that you have a ring, too. And I don't know what any of it means. Can you call me?"

Now all she could do was sleep. Just sleep. Sleep was good.

* * *

Micky shook her awake. She was standing next to the bed, still clutching the little wax figure in her hand. "My stomach hurts," she said. "I feel ever so sick."

Claire opened her eyes, tried to focus on her sister's face closing in on hers. "Tell mum. She'll sort you."

"She's being sick. She said to get you. I feel ever so hot." Micky had hold of Claire's hand and was pressing it against her forehead.

She does feel hot, Claire thought. *Really hot.*

"Okay. I'm coming." She sat up, still holding Micky's hand, which felt clammy, and swung her legs over the side of the bed. "Let's go and see how Mum is."

For a second, Claire just stood in the doorway and looked at her mum rolling around the bed, clutching at her stomach and moaning. "Mum?" Claire was beside her now.

"Oh God, Claire," she whispered. "It feels like I've got ants crawling all over me. My tongue's tingling. It's so weird. I feel really weird."

"Shall I get you some paracetamol?"

"No good," her mum whispered. "Can't keep it down." Her eyes started to roll up into her head and she was making a noise as if she had swallowed her tongue and was choking on it.

Micky crawled onto the bed and buried her face in her mum's side. She was wailing horribly. A high-pitched, grizzling, liquid noise that set Claire's every nerve on edge.

"I need to get a doctor," Claire was muttering to herself. They hadn't registered with one yet, so she would need to call Grandma's old one, though she knew in her heart that it was too late for that. Her mind just didn't want to accept it. "Number. Number. Where's the number?"

She ran downstairs and started scrabbling

around in the hall table drawer, looking for Grandma's address book. It wasn't there. But the more she panicked, the worse things got. She flicked desperately through the Yellow Pages, her mind a blank. Name? She couldn't remember the doctor's name. Would her mum be able to tell her? Back upstairs she looked down at her mum lying there, her face all sunken and grey. And Micky had stopped crying and her breathing was ragged and harsh.

Claire picked up the phone and called 999. Seven minutes. The ambulance would be there in seven minutes. Bear with them... the services were very stretched. She rang her dad's number, then his mobile. No reply.

She ought to stay with her mum and Micky. But she couldn't bear to. Terrified she would look down at them and know it was too late and they were both dead.

She mustn't think about that. She'd go and open the front door instead. At least she'd be ready when the ambulance came. But, oh God, there on the step was a black rat, stiff and cold with a trickle of blood coming from its nose. She shuddered and pushed it away with her foot. Then she saw another, lying on its back at the side of the path; its eyes closed, its mouth open in a perfect 'O' and its tiny paws stiff and supplicant as if it were praying.

She ran back upstairs now and looked helplessly at her mum and Micky. Then she started to cry, whispering, "Please, please, please," over and over. She took her mum's hand and it felt cold. "Please don't be dead. Please don't be dead." Anger and frustration and hate started to bubble up inside her. Her dad. Why wasn't he here? Where was he? Then she heard a voice call out in the hall. She ran to the top of the stairs.

"Claire?"

The relief of seeing someone, *anyone*, was just so great that she didn't stop to ask what he, Robert, was doing there. And anyway the ambulance arrived then and everything was forgotten in the rush to get her mum and Micky, still clutching her wax doll, onto stretchers and into the ambulance.

Claire would have climbed in as well, but the ambulance men were firm. No room, they said. They looked at *him* standing close beside her, his hand on her elbow, supporting, restraining.

"Don't worry," he said. "I'll take her." She ought to have done something then. Taken control. Got a taxi to take her to the hospital. But she didn't. Felt… and it seemed ridiculous later… that it would be impolite to refuse his help, even though he made her feel afraid. So they stood together, on the pavement, in the pool of light from the street lamp. And watched as the ambulance doors were shut and the ambulance, blue light flashing, pulled away. Then Robert turned to her and asked if there was anything that needed to be fetched from the house.

"My backpack," she whispered, still in a daze. "Can I have it? It's under the kitchen table, I think. It's got my phone in it. Oh, and mum's handbag. Upstairs by her bed. "

Her mum never went anywhere without her bag. Everything went into it. Everything. Even the little wax doll.

"I'll get them. You sit in the car."

She allowed herself to be tucked up in the passenger seat. "And keys. On the hall table…"

He disappeared into the house and came out just a few minutes later, carrying both bags and locking the door behind him. She saw him stop on the path; look down at where the rats were lying. He pushed one with the toe of his shoe. He was still smiling when he slid into the driver's seat.

* * *

The journey to the hospital only took five minutes. There was very little traffic that late at night. But every one of those minutes felt like ten. And when they stopped at a red traffic light she cried out in frustration and hit at the dashboard with her fist.

He reached across and rested his hand on hers. It felt heavy. Hot and dry and heavy. She kept her eyes fixed ahead. "Do you think they are going to die?" she asked.

He took his hand away and said nothing and they drove on in silence, until at last they pulled up outside the hospital entrance. He leaned across her to push open the passenger door. She pressed herself back into the seat; held her breath, not wanting to breathe in the smell of him.

"You go in," he said. "I'll find somewhere to park."

She jumped out, clutching her backpack.

"Wait!" Her mum's bag. He was holding it out for her. She took it and slammed the door shut. He drove off. She felt the relief of it turn her legs to water.

* * *

Accident and Emergency. She had never seen one this busy before. And they'd been loads of times to the one near her old house. Micky always seemed to be breaking things; a toe, a leg, a finger. Always falling out of trees, off her skateboard or bike.

It was totally manic. People everywhere. Noise. Bright fluorescent light. She had no idea what to do. There was a reception desk, but the woman behind it was harassed, didn't listen to what Claire was saying, told her to take a ticket from the machine, sit down and wait her turn. Claire tried to say that it was her mum and sister who were the patients, but the woman was on the phone now and shooed her away with a hand. Claire took a ticket. Number 45. But a nurse had only just called out 38.

She went and sat down on the only spare seat, between a woman with a black eye and a man nursing a clumsily bandaged hand, dripping blood, and sat there in a daze. Her arms and legs felt heavy. She could hardly move them. A headache was starting. The top of her skull was so sensitive that even touching it with the tips of her fingers was painful. Her throat was tightening up. Her eyes felt dry and sore. She looked up at the clock on the wall. Two minutes past midnight. She registered that it was now officially her birthday, and that *he* was taking a long time to park the car. Perhaps he'd gone home and left her? Yes! But how would she get home if he had? She didn't have more than a couple of pounds and her mum never had much either, using her card to pay for everything. She wanted her dad. That was all she could think of. An adult to come and lift the weight of responsibility off her shoulders. It was too heavy. She didn't want it. Wasn't old enough, even at 14, to take it.

"Forty-five. Number forty-five!" Someone was calling out her number. She held up her hand. Half stood up. A nurse holding a clipboard was threading her way towards her. Claire sank back down onto her seat and let the nurse come and hunker down beside her. She was brisk and efficient. As soon as Claire told her the story, she took down her mum and her sister's names. Told

Claire she'd go and find out what was happening to them and come back when she knew anything. She stood up, patting Claire on the shoulder and telling her not to worry. She was sure everything would be fine.

Claire thought about ringing her dad again. She took her mobile out of her backpack. But she ought to go outside to do that. And supposing the nurse came back then and couldn't find her? No one was looking. She'd send a text. She checked there was a signal then surreptitiously keyed in '*At hospital. Urgent. Call me.*' She tried to send it, but the screen just flashed '*Message sending failed*'. Oh no. She slipped the phone into her jeans back pocket. And soon the nurse was back and carrying the little wax doll they'd had to prise, she said, from Micky's hand. "Better if you look after it," she said, with a shudder. "Gives me the creeps."

Claire was sitting there clutching it, when *Robert* came.

"There weren't any spaces. I had to drive round for ages before I could find somewhere." And while he was talking, he took the wax doll out of her hand. "See. It's melting in the heat. It's all squashed now. No use at all." He pocketed it.

Good. He could have her mum's too. Before it melted and made a mess. Claire unzipped her mum's bag. Fished around inside. But there was no wax doll.

"Never mind," he said. "It helped."

Helped? What *was* he talking about? Her mum and her sister had nearly died.

"Has anything happened yet?" he said calmly. "Is there any news?"

* * *

It wasn't until two in the morning that the nurse was able to tell them anything. She'd taken Claire and Robert into a side room and was sitting opposite Claire and leaning in towards her and looking earnestly into her eyes.

"It's not bird flu. That's for certain. We think it's some sort of poison, but we don't know what yet. I shouldn't tell you this." She looked a bit embarrassed. "But the doctor Googled the symptoms and they're a perfect fit for aconite poisoning. But that's incredibly rare. Is there anywhere they could have come across it?" Now the nurse was looking up at Robert, who was standing close behind Claire's chair.

It couldn't have been *his* 'medicine', could it? Had he given some to her mum and Micky? Should she say something? She could feel his hand resting on her shoulder. Just the touch of his fingers, but enough to make her feel afraid. He shook his head.

"We stomach-pumped them both, just to be on the safe side. And we've given them the antidote for aconite."

She could feel Robert's thumb pressing in on her neck; his fingers fan out over her collar bone.

"But it will take a few hours yet for it to work. After that we'll move them up into the wards. You can come in and see them now, if you like. But then I'd go home if I were you. Have you got hold of your dad yet?"

Manuscript 8

My mother never did wake again. Though Nicholas lifted her up and carried her back to the house. Though he gave her more of his medicine and bled her copiously.

I watched as the life drained out of her and felt a terrible pain in my heart at it. My mother, the very last of my flesh and blood. For my brother had died at birth and I had no aunts or uncles that I knew of, no grandparents for they were long dead.

"If only we had the 21st spell, Margrat, then we might bring her back to life again," he sighed, "But it is not time yet..."

"And no one has the em..." I quickly swallowed my words. I had never heard Nicholas talk of the Emerald Casket, and did not want him to hear of it from me, or know more of my meeting with Christophe.

෨෧ ෧෨

Now my mother was dead, Nicholas and I dug her grave together and she was buried alongside my father. In the darkness I faced the stark truth. I was alone and had no one to care for me.

But it seemed that Nicholas thought differently, saying, the very minute we were out of the black, suffocating heat of the cellar, that I must leave the house and go with him. "It is not safe for you to stay here Margrat... a young girl, all alone. Besides..."And this is when he told me, "Your mother has left a will making me your guardian."

I said that I did not believe him.

He took me into the parlour then and, with a key he took from his pocket, opened the box seat of my mother's oak chair. Inside was a will, written in her hand... I knew it well... and bearing her true signature, Catherine Jennet. It was dated the third day of September. Just yesterday.

Nicholas watched me as I picked up the will, let it curl back into a roll. Was quick to stay my hand as, seeing a candle still alight on the mantlepiece, I thought to catch the will in the flame and burn it.

There was no time to pack. Nicholas was in a hurry to be gone. Besides, he said, it was dangerous to take clothing and linens and the like, for they might harbour infection. Though I noticed that he was careful to tuck the will inside his coat. "No Margrat, you shall have all new things."

New things. Once I would have danced and sung and clapped my hands in glee at the thought of it.

So I left the house with nothing but the clothes I stood up in and the ring still on its thread about my neck.

"I think it safer," he said, as we stepped out into the lane, "if we go by the river."

So we went, Nicholas holding my hand tight, not by the Ludgate, but on foot down St Peter's Hill to Poles Wharf. All the while Nicholas looking about him.

"Who or what is it you are afraid of?" I asked, breathless, for he pulled me along at a great rate. "Not… the rope-walker… for he must have left the city."

He did not answer, but gripped my hand more tightly and would not even let go when I stumbled and fell to my knees. Instead he pulled me up so sharply I yelped in pain. And it wasn't until we reached the wharf and Nicholas was handing me down into a wherry that I looked back and saw Christophe. I am sure it was he, though he slipped from view as Nicholas took one last look about him and then jumped down into the boat.

I had not been out on the river for a long time. But it seemed busier than ever now. The waterman told us that many people, hoping to be spared the plague, had abandoned their houses and were living, whole families squeezed together, on boats. We passed many of these, at anchor in midstream and in rows of two or three or more together. The waterman rowed us on up, past Bridewell and the cloisters of Whitefriars. Midday now. The bells rang out across the water and the sun blazed down. The creak of the boat's timbers, the rhythmic swish of the oars and the glitter and glint off the water, made me feel light-headed.

On past the great houses of Essex Place and Arundel Place and to Somerset House and its river stairs. The waterman expertly brought us in, shipped his oars and jumped out onto the wharf side to tie up. Nicholas jumped out himself and turned and held out his hand for me, pulling me up.

A lane led up from the river, alongside the garden wall of a big house. We went along it, Nicholas holding my hand still. Then we passed into the Strand.

A little way down and set well back, we came to Nicholas's house. It was three storeys high, brick-built and very fine, its many windows glittering in the bright September light. Plaster panels set between them, decorated in relief, with what I saw at once were Egyptian figures. It was different in every way from my own house, which was built of daub and wattle and had grown higgledy-piggledy over a great many years, with no clear plan in view. The architect of this house had a mind that was controlled and clear of purpose.

I straggled after the Doctor as he went up the front steps. Taking a key from his coat pocket, he unlocked the great carved oak door. It swung open and I followed Nicholas into blackness; for all the shutters were closed and there were no candles lit.

It had been hot as an oven outside. Now the cold struck up through the stone floor and made me shiver.

It is like a tomb, I thought. And even when Nicholas folded back the shutters and light flooded in, the chill remained. Now I could see that there was panelling to the walls and fine plaster moulding on the ceiling. There was an immense chimney piece with pillars of jet, but no fire lit.

It had the feel of a mausoleum. And there were no

servants anywhere to be seen. They must have all run away, I thought, like Jane. There was a carved oak chair by the fireplace. I sat down heavily upon it. I looked down at my filthy skirts, my muddied shoes; at my hands grimed with black. I had not washed or changed my clothes or cleaned my teeth for days and days. And I had not noticed that I stank, until now, for the whole world had smelled the same.

"You need to bathe," Nicholas said, as if reading my mind. "I have clean clothes already laid out upon your bed."

My bed...

"Come..." He held out his hand and I let him pull me up. For what else could I do? What other choices did I have?

We walked up the wide oak staircase and he showed me the room that was to be my bedchamber with its high carved bed and silk-embroidered hangings. There were tapestries on the walls and richly patterned carpets on the floor. A basin and ewer filled with clean water stood on a chest. Soap that smelled sweetly of roses and honeysuckle. Fine linens to dry myself. A tortoiseshell comb and looking glass in a frame embroidered with flowers. Toothpowder, hair curling papers and perfumes. And laid out on the bed, the finest cotton shift, trimmed with lace. A skirt and bodice in silk taffeta; soft mourning grey, the colour of a pigeon's wing. Beautiful, beautiful things.

Then, when I was left alone and I had stepped out of my old clothes and I was quite naked, except for the braid and the ring, I took up the mirror and looked in it and hardly knew myself. For the child Margrat had gone and could never come back now.

I washed slowly and carefully. I dried myself; breathed in the heady smell of roses and honeysuckle. I combed my hair until it shone and rippled over my shoulders like liquid bronze. I took the shift from the bed and let it drop over my head. I pulled on the skirt and laced up the bodice. I slipped stockinged feet into buckled and embroidered shoes. All fitted perfectly... as if he had the measure of me already.

Then I walked from the room and down the stairs and into my new life.

ৡৡ৯৯

I had been wrong in believing there were no servants. There was one. She served us that first day at table. She was a slight, mousy-haired girl, who scurried about bringing in dishes of meats and bread and salads; filling our glasses with wine and saying nothing above a whisper. A timid-seeming little thing, who quivered when the Doctor spoke to her.

Her name was Martha, but I never did find out much else about her, all the time I was there. Except I might trust her with my life.

She flitted about the house from sunrise to sunset, keeping the sea coals banked up in the fires, the floors swept and dusting all the many curios the Doctor had collected on his travels: pottery from ancient Athens. Marble statues from Rome. Exquisitely illuminated manuscripts. Wall hangings. One of St George slaying the Dragon, that always made me stop and look up at it. Then there were the books. On all manner of subjects: philosophy, theology, medicine, alchemy, the magic arts.

And Nefertaru.

It had been a shock to see her mummy case standing in the far corner of the library, for I had thought she was still on show at the Head and Combe. Now she was a constant reminder of things I wished to forget, so I kept away from the library.

But there was one room that was never swept or dusted. It was Nicholas's study on the second floor of the house, directly above my bedchamber and with the same view over the Strand. He kept it locked at all *times, even when he was at work there. Which I quickly noticed followed a pattern. He rose early, before dawn, and said prayers in his study. I could hear the steady rise and fall of his voice and I knew that he burned incense, for the house filled with its bittersweet smell. Cassia, myrrh, aloes – the sweet smell, so the Bible tells, of our Lord Jesus.*

Then after breakfast, he went out and often did not return until late afternoon. I know that he went to purchase herbs brought ashore at Fresh Wharf. I believe he was also physician to a number of high-born people. What else he did, I was never sure but sometimes, when he came home, he brought presents for me: shoes and a beautiful silver necklace to thread the ring through, as he feared the red braid might fray and break.

No visitors ever called at the house. I thought that strange. I saw no one but Nicholas and Martha. No, that is not true, for I watched the world from my bedroom window. And one morning I saw Christophe. Or thought I saw him.

I opened the window, leaned out, called his name (Nicholas had gone out early or I would not have dared do it). But whoever it was did not turn around and had soon disappeared into Little Drury Lane.

At first I was wary of Nicholas, though I felt such

an attraction to him. Perhaps that was why I asked if Martha might sleep on a truckle in my bedchamber. But Nicholas said she went home at night. So I kept my door locked instead and the candle burning. I listened for footsteps on the stair, the turn of the doorknob, hushed breathing. I fell into a troubled sleep, haunted by the ghosts of my dead father and mother. I dreamed of them; they were running through the streets and alleyways, just ahead of me and forever out of reach. I would wake at first light, in tears and to the sound of the Nicholas's prayers, the smell of his incense enveloping me, but the door still locked and the candle gone out.

So it was that those first few weeks drifted by. Nicholas did nothing to make me feel uneasy. He said nothing about the Book of Thoth or Sekhmet. Nothing about the spell. And if I worried he might know of the Emerald Casket, he said nothing that made me fearful. It was as if he had forgotten all about the 21st spell, or was reconciled to its loss.

I confess, in believing that, I was stupid and naive. I ought to have observed him more carefully. Then I would have seen that he never forgot the smallest thing nor was ever reconciled to anything, not even the loss of a waistcoat button. But he seemed a quite different man then; more vibrant, more alive. It made me think of my mother. How, as the great feast day of Christmas approached, her mood always lightened. She sang and laughed and danced about the house and my father said she became again, just for that short while, the girl he had married.

I was gulled by him. Utterly taken in. Seduced. The powerful attraction I felt for him, but which had till then been tempered by fear, now began to consume me. I took his name, Nicholas, and wrote it out endlessly. Whispered it to myself over and over. When he was away from me, I felt as if I was a fire struggling to stay alight. When he was there, the sight, the sound, the smell and touch of him, fanned that fire into an inferno. In the evenings, before the light had faded, he would read aloud to me. The poetry of Shakespeare, Herrick, Milton. Tales from Ancient Greece and Egypt and his own translations. Magical stories, brilliantly told.

Then with all the candles lit, though there was no one to play for us and no others to make up the set, he would ask me to dance. I could not refuse him. And so, anyone looking in on us, would have seen a strange sight. A tall, dark-haired man and a small, flame-haired young woman circling solemnly about each other. No sound except the slip and click of our shoes on the polished floor.

How beautiful he seemed to me then as he began slowly to bind me to him; with ropes as fine but as strong as gossamer. If I had once thought of running from him, I no longer saw the need to do so. If I was held prisoner, then I could not see it. If the door to my cell had been left open wide, I should have stayed inside and thrown away the key. I have heard since that this sometimes happens: the prisoner comes to love his prison and his gaoler.

So one day rolled into the next, with little variation. Except... one morning I was woken with a griping pain in my belly. Getting out of bed to use the chamber pot and lifting my nightshirt, I saw blood trickling down between my legs. I stopped a droplet with my finger and looked at it in shock. I knew what it was, for my mother had told me about it. A monthly show of blood signifying that I was now a grown woman and ready to conceive and bear a child.

I sat down heavily on the bed, my legs trembling. I was careless of the blood seeping through my nightshirt and onto the coverlet. I felt a tear run hot down my cheek and then another and then another. I felt a great sob rise up and break free. Soon my whole body was wracked with them. And that was how Martha found me and she said nothing, but her eyes took in the red stains on the nightshirt and the coverlet. She came and put her arms around me. Tentatively at first, but then as I clung to her, she stroked my hair and whispered soft words and rocked me like the child a part of me still wished to be. Once I was calmer, she went and put the wash basin on the floor and fetched hot water and poured it in. She held out the cake of soap and I took it and, crouching over the basin, started to wash the blood away. It swirled in the water like red smoke and soon the water was the colour of a brilliant sunset. I wiped myself with a linen cloth and, though I had washed carefully, blood still stained it. Then she showed me how to take a strip of linen, fold it and fasten it with pins to the gusset of my drawers.

✦

Nicholas came to my bedchamber later that morning. But I would not open the door to him, though he spoke softly to me. For I was both proud that I was now a grown woman and yet ashamed. "I will leave some laudanum for you. It will ease the discomfort and do you no harm."

When I was sure he had gone, I opened the door and took in the medicine. Laudanum. My mother had given it to me when I had the toothache. It had taken away the pain and made me sleep. I could still remember its taste. Bitter and sweet together. Opium and sherry wine. I unstopped the blue glass bottle and poured out a spoonful. I hesitated for a moment, then putting the spoon to my lips, let the sticky liquid trickle down my throat. I felt its warmth spreading out through my body. Just one spoonful could do no harm. I would take no more until I could see what its effects might be.

Soon I began to feel peaceful and at ease. I lay down on the bed and with the griping in my belly soothed, I fell asleep.

❧

When I woke up again, night was falling. One spoonful of laudanum and I had lost the whole of a day. But the pain had gone and I felt calmer than I had felt for a very long time. Yet when Nicholas came to my door that evening and asked if I would come down to supper, I still refused him. "I cannot," I said, remembering what my mother had said. "For I will turn the wine sour."

"And will you turn the pickled meat rancid and curdle the milk too? Old wives' tales, Margrat. You should not heed them!"

But I did and it was four days before the flow of blood stopped and I could allow myself to get up and get dressed and go downstairs again.

And when I first sat down again to supper with Nicholas, I knew something had subtly changed between us. That night, when I went to my bed, I did not lock the bedchamber door. I fell into a feverish sleep. And when I awoke and found him standing over me, I felt no surprise or fear. There was just an agony of longing, which only increased when he lay down beside me, but not at first touching. I could feel his breath, hear my own heartbeat loud in my ears. He said nothing and there was nothing to say.

His fingers undoing the ribbon at the neck of my nightgown, brushed against my collarbone. His hand, slipping around my waist, found the hollow of my back and pressed me in close. The heat of our bodies; the sweet musky smell of mine and the sharp smell of his. And I thought: this is what it must be like to die a little death and then to come back to life again and fly out in a thousand tiny pieces. The shape of his hands, the curve of his mouth, the way his skin felt like silk and his hair fell and curled against his shoulder. All those things drew me in, but it was his mind that held me. The naked power of it. And all the while I told myself I would not be utterly lost to him. That I would keep some part of myself safe and hidden from him. But it was like a drug. An addiction. There was always the need for more. And with each night, the recklessness increased. Now he would come and stay just a little while. He lay close to me, whispering my name and stroking my hair. Nothing more. After he left my mind would be in such disorder that I could not sleep. And I grew so desperate to find some peace that I fell to taking laudanum each evening.

Then, one night in early December, when the fire was lit in the grate and the frost was thick on the windowpane, he came and did not leave. And for a few sweet hours before dawn, I learned how it was possible to exist outside of time and in a place that is all pleasure and sensation.

When I awoke, just before first light, he was there still, lying beside me. How peaceful he looked. How vulnerable he seemed as he slept. But as I watched, his eyes flew open and widened for a second, as if in fear. But then he blinked and the fear was gone and he was wholly himself again. I reached out and touched his mouth. He took my hand and kissed its palm, then folded my fingers over and held it in his. He told me that I would soon be his for ever. And I felt weak at the thought of it. We were together every night after that, though he was always gone before sunrise. Even on the morning of the 23rd day of December… my 14th birthday.

Martha came with a present, a cake she had made herself and with my name pricked out in currants on the top. I washed and dressed hurriedly and went down to breakfast, but I ate alone. I asked Martha where he had gone, but she did not know.

⟨෧෧෧⟩

I was almost asleep by the fire in the parlour when he appeared. He was carrying something wrapped in a gold brocade cloth. He placed the parcel in my lap. It felt very light.

I looked up at him. Though he looked calm, I felt excitement burning inside him, as clearly as I felt the heat from the fire on my cheek. Whatever it was he had brought for me must be very special. I unwrapped the parcel quickly. The brocade fell back and there was a casket. An emerald-green casket. I knew at once what it must be. My hands trembled, my mind was like snow.

Now he was kneeling beside me. His hands reached around my neck and he undid the silver necklace. Slipped off the ring and began to push it onto the third finger of my right hand. I was afraid, confused, for hadn't he told me not to wear it on pain of death? And worse, when the ring would not even squeeze past the first joint, he grew very angry. His eyes glittered like jet. I could see the muscles around his jaw tighten and the veins in his neck stand out. "It will not matter," he said fiercely, "the little finger will do…"

"Look, look!" I said. "It will fit. I know it… there… it is loose and I will have to take care not to lose it, but it will fit. See how easily it does…" Now the fire of his anger grew white hot and fear of what he might do – a desperate need to dampen down his anger – was making me gabble.

His hand was against my mouth and with the other, he pressed the ring on my little finger into the cartouche on the box. I sat stock-still, rigid with fear and hardly daring to breathe. His hand was crushing mine. Tighter and tighter until I could hear the bones crack. Rage, sorrow, bewilderment; all these emotions passing across his face as quick as the blink of an eye. He seemed to have forgotten that I was there. He was muttering to himself, repeating words over and over, as if by saying them out loud he might come to some better understanding of them. Which all at once he seemed to do, for he grew calmer. He loosened his grip on me and his eyes focused in on my face. His hand reached up and stroked my cheek. He smiled, saying, "The one true daughter. Now I see what it means…"

I did not. But at least whatever was in the casket was safe. The ring was not the key to opening it. Nicholas and Christophe were both mistaken.

⁓⊙⊙⁓

At first I did not know that anything was amiss. I had only just begun to menstruate and so when several months passed with no bleeding, I paid it no attention. But then I began to thicken around the waist and my clothes became uncomfortably tight. In the mornings I would wake up and be violently sick. Even a further dose of laudanum would not relieve it. I knew what it meant now, for Martha had told me that I must be with child.

I was mortally afraid of what Nicholas would say. But I need not have worried, for instead of raging at my news, he seemed overjoyed, saying she, the baby growing inside me, would have her mother's red hair and her father's single-mindedness of purpose.

When I said he could not know it would be a daughter, he smiled at me as if I were an innocent, "Only a daughter can be brought to term and live. Any male child of my bloodline will die in the womb or be stillborn. The spells have given me power over that at least."

My mind refused to admit the true horror of what he was saying. But my arms crossed low round my belly as if to protect the baby inside me... though I knew such a gesture was futile. I prayed with all my heart that I would be safely delivered of a girl, with hair the dull brown of a field mouse. That Nicholas would forget his obsession with opening the casket. But my prayers went unanswered.

∂℘ ℘∂

As the months passed and my belly swelled and I did not miscarry, he became ever more jubilant. It was as if we had been incomplete in ourselves and were now made whole. When he was absent, my thoughts were always with him. When he was there, his eyes were always upon me. Winter slowly turned to spring.

The weather, at first warm, became wet and foul. The Doctor rarely went out now. He watched over me. Carefully. But on the 23rd day of April, St George's Day, he was absent from the house. He must go, he said, to attend the anniversary of the King's Coronation at the Palace of Westminster. But before he went he placed a hand on my belly and said words in a language I had never heard spoken before.

From the window of my bedchamber, I watched him climb into the carriage and drive away. I stood for a long time looking down into the street. My hands resting on the swell of my five-month belly, tight like a drum. Then I felt a fluttering inside, as if my stomach was full of moths, some discomfort and an urgent need to push down, as if I might squeeze out the baby growing inside me. Which I silently did.

Moments later, lifting my skirts and obeying that urge to push, I was delivered of it. Still in its caul, which was supple like fine leather, slippery as soap and clear as frosted glass. I could see the baby curled up and floating inside it. Thinking, in my ignorance, that I might save it, I tore open the sack with my fingers, the warm waters gushing out. Then I sat back in shock at the sight of it. Its body so small it would fit into the palm of my hand. Its eyes not yet open, but fused over.

So mesmerised was I by it, I did not notice Martha come into the room. It was only when she knelt down beside me, took out a knife from her apron pocket and bent towards the baby, that I was jolted out of my reverie.

"No!" I cried out, not understanding what it was she meant to do. But she pushed me gently away, saying, "Shh now. I mean only to cut the cord. See, it is a boy. There now, you shall hold him for a while." Which I did, taking in every little thing about him. The tiny hands and toes with their perfect nails all in miniature. The translucence of his skin, with the map of his veins showing clearly through.

"Now, mistress." She took him from me and wrapped him in her apron.

"You must bury him for me in the orchard, and say a blessing." I held her by the arm and looked beseechingly into her eyes.

"I will. But first we must clean you up and all this too."

I looked down at the floor which was wet and bloody. The afterbirth lay there, looking for all the world like so much raw offal laid out on a butcher's stall.

๏๛

Nicholas returned home late. I had been watching for him out of the window. Though the city was all aglow from the light of the bonfires celebrating the king's anniversary, I got no pleasure at all from the sight. I could only think of my baby buried now in the orchard, and of what Nicholas would say when he knew what had happened. I was sure he would be angry with me. I had failed him. A son, and not the daughter he seemed to long for.

At last I saw him; heard his foot on the stairs and I went out to him. I must have fainted then, for when I awoke, I was in my bed and he was there, sitting beside me. "He..."

"Shh. There will be others." He reached for the bottle of laudanum which was on the chair by the bed. And I dutifully took three spoonfuls. He stroked my brow until I fell asleep.

Chapter 9

It had seemed the only thing to do. Robert had said that he would drive her across London to her old house. Then she would know whether her dad was there or not. And if he wasn't, she could leave him a note and then he, Robert, would drive her back again. So that is what she wanted to believe would happen.

But then they had crossed over the river and were heading along Pimlico Road when he said, "There's something I must sort out first. It won't take long. My house isn't far away."

What could she say? It didn't feel right, but then nothing did just now. The whole world seemed about to collapse around her in terrifying chaos. Her anxiety levels were off the scale. Three in the morning. She'd never been out that late without her mum and dad. Now she was with a man she really knew nothing about, except he wanted something very badly and she was the key. Well, she would stay in the car while he went into the house. That would be the safest thing to do.

And when they arrived, pulled up outside that house, he said, as if he knew what she was thinking, "You can stay in the car if you like. I won't be long. But keep the doors locked and sound the horn if you get scared. You never know who's around this time of night."

So she sat in the car, terrified. And the fear made her want to pee. She needed to distract herself. Took out her mobile and tried her dad again. A signal this time, but his phone was still off. She'd started to ring Zacharie, but stopped. Didn't want to wake him… and anyway, what did she expect him to do? Now the need to pee was becoming urgent. Painful. She could get out of the car and use the gutter. But supposing someone came… found her with her knickers down around her ankles. Vulnerable. She looked out of the car window and thought she saw someone, small and slight, slipping into the alleyway that ran alongside the house.

She tried to hold on, but now she was desperate. So desperate that it blocked out the fear and in seconds she was banging on the door to be let in. But when she ran to use the cloakroom downstairs, he stopped her, saying the toilet was blocked and she would have to use the bathroom on the top floor.

She was bursting, so she ran up the stairs after him, even though every nerve ending in her body was screaming out; telling her not to go.

"You look worn out," he said, pushing open the bathroom door and turning on the light. "If you want to have a wash…" She pushed past him and slammed the door in his face, locking it.

She tore down her jeans and knickers and sat down on the loo. And for a second nothing happened and then… oh, the relief of it… and she was able to look around. Notice there were clean towels laid out on the side of the bath. A new toothbrush and toothpaste. A round cake of soap, smelling of honeysuckle and roses. She would have given anything to have a shower. Strip off her dirty, sweaty clothes and stand under a stream of hot, pure water. But even with the door locked she didn't feel safe. So she just pulled up her jeans, flushed the toilet and then washed her hands and splashed water on her face. She felt better now.

Calmer. Was able to say to herself: "Bad things happen to other people" and almost believe it.

So when she came out and saw that the door to the room next door was ajar, she couldn't stop herself from pushing it open. *Just a quick look,* she thought, and because it was still dark outside, her hand automatically searched for the light switch. But the room was lit already... with candles, though they had burned down a long way and the draught of air as she had pushed open the door had made a few of them gutter and then go out. The light in the room was hazy with their smoke. And it was hot. Unbearably hot. She could feel a trickle of sweat run down the side of her forehead. She brushed it away.

At the far side of the room was a four-poster bed, hung with heavy silk curtains. She crept closer to have a look and could see now that there were clothes laid out on it. She dropped her backpack down at the foot of the bed and reached out to touch them. The grey silk dress and the fine cotton petticoat smelling of roses and honeysuckle. And the little shoes. Oh, the shoes were beautiful. Pale grey silk. She had never seen anything like them before. She reached out to touch their glittering silver buckles and trace the outline of the flowers exquisitely embroidered on them.

He must have been watching her as she moved about the room, stopping to look and to touch anything that caught her interest. But she hadn't known he was there. Waiting. Not until she stopped at the table near to the shuttered window, laid out with combs, a looking glass and a silver necklace, thick and heavy as rope. Not until she had picked up the necklace, threading it through her fingers, coiling it, smooth and cool, sinuous as a snake, into her palm.

"Seventeenth century," he said, reaching a hand over her shoulder and making her start. Then, before she could stop him, he had taken the necklace, looped it round her neck and, pushing her hair up out of the way, had fastened the catch. "There." He turned her to face him. "A present for your birthday, just gone."

She was going to say that she didn't want it. Her hands were already fumbling with the catch.

But then he said something that stopped her dead in her tracks. "It was Margrat's. Now you must wear it." He held up the looking glass. "See how beautiful you look. The image of her."

He reached inside his jacket and taking out a tiny oval miniature, held it out.

Claire didn't want to look at it. She was afraid of what she might see. But she felt compelled to take it.

"I had so little time," he was smiling, "but I did well, don't you think? It is a very good likeness. I have caught exactly the colour of her eyes and hair."

Claire's eyes and hair too. Her hand shook uncontrollably. She was alone in a house with a man who clearly believed he had known a woman alive over four hundred years ago. He was mad. He had to be. What other explanation was there?

He held out his hand to take back the miniature. She would give it back and then sprint for the door. It was still half open. Then she could be down the stairs and out and running until she reached safety. So she held out the miniature, but instead of taking it, he grabbed her wrist and squeezed it so tight Claire could feel her fingers throbbing. The ring burned so hot now on her finger, it seemed almost to glow against the paleness of her skin. The miniature fell to the floor.

Now he'll let me go, she thought. *So he can pick it up.*

But he didn't. Quite calmly and not dropping his eyes from hers, even for a second, he stepped on it. Deliberately. Ground his heel into it, destroying it completely. "I do not need her, now I have you... the one true daughter, the key to opening the Emerald Casket at last."

Manuscript 9

The loss of my baby weighed heavy on me. I took more laudanum to dull the pain. Though Nicholas came to my bed each night, I took no pleasure in it now. He always left before first light and then I would sleep, on and on, sometimes not leaving my bed at all for days on end. It felt for all the world as if I was entombed in a dull, grey heavy leaden casket and I would never escape from it. Martha brought food and drink, but she had to coax me to eat, even a little. And while she coaxed and cajoled, she prattled and it was she that told me fewer people were dying of the plague now.

"As if I care anything about that, when my mother and father and baby son are already dead," I hissed, turning away from her and pulling the covers even further over my head. But I could not help but think of what she had said; that fewer were dying. So perhaps Sekhmet's plague dogs had gone, knowing that my ring

would not unlock the casket and the spell was safe. Now the very tiniest spark of a will to live and to escape this terrible feeling of numbness leaped up inside me.

But even though I did then rise from my bed and wash and dress myself, I was in danger of slipping back into the dream world I had wilfully constructed about me. Of believing that Nicholas did truly love me for myself and not for the daughter he hoped I would bear him. For did not the proof of his love lie in everything he did? How he had made a miniature portrait of me and carried it everywhere with him, close to his heart. How he was so solicitous of me. How he flew into a rage and struck me across the face when he found me at the open door and about to step into the street. How he was immediately sorry for that and took me at once in his arms and kissed away my tears and promised never to strike me again. Which he never did. Above once.

And perhaps I would have slipped back down into that world, if, one morning in early March, a boy had not come to the door with an urgent message for the Doctor.

"The yard is all on fire sir. All your herbs and medicines are gone up in smoke."

Nicholas left in a great hurry.

Now, in all the months I had lived in the house, I had never once been inside his study. Nicholas had made it clear that I might go anywhere in the house, except that one room. And in case I should be tempted, the door was always locked. But when I passed it that morning, the door was ajar and I could not resist the temptation to turn the handle and go in.

It was a room in size, the same as my own. But it seemed much smaller, for every wall was shelved from floor to ceiling. And on the shelves were hundreds of boxes and jars. Their labels were written in Nicholas's clear script and in both Latin and English. There were books too, astrological charts and a desk with a microscope, weighing scales and a pestle and mortar set out on it.

So this was where he prepared his medicines and burned his incense. I could feel the smell of it entering into the very weave of my clothes and into every pore of my skin. I read the titles of the books: The Pharmacopoeia. The Complete Herbal and English Physician. The Book of Poisons. *And the labels on some of the jars: Antimony. Hemlock. Distillation of Aconite – in a blue glass bottle. I unstopped it and took a sniff, though I did not dare taste what was inside.*

Then one bottle caught my eye. It looked to be full of the same liquid the Doctor had prepared for my parents. I took it down and read the label. ARISTOLOCHIA. Snake root. Took out the stopper and sniffing it, recognised it as the 'plague water' Nicholas had given to my mother and father.

Well whatever it was, I thought, it had not saved my parents from the plague and death. But I was curious about it. Taking the Herbal *from the shelf, I turned the pages until I came to a description of it. And ever after wished I had not...*

Used sparingly, a stimulant. In excess a poison, causing violent irritations of the stomach, vomiting, paralysis of the lungs and coma followed by death.

Excess. Was two spoonfuls day after day an excess? If so, then my parents had not died of the plague as I had thought, but had been poisoned. And I, unwittingly had given the last dose of it to my mother. The book slipped from my hands and fell to the floor.

I do not know how long I might have stood there if Martha had not found me.

"You should not have come in here," she whispered. I knew that.

She bent and picked up the Herbal, *wiped it clean of dust and placed it back on the shelf. She took my hand and led me out of the study. She closed the door behind us. "You must pray that he never finds out."*

I did pray. But it was in vain, for the minute he returned and came to find me, he knew. He stepped close. Too close. He could smell the incense and the fear. I struggled to keep my voice calm. I confessed I had peeked in at the door. It had been open, I said, and curiosity had overcome me. I had not touched anything. I swore on everything that was holy, I was telling the truth. He pinched my chin between his thumb and forefinger and tilted my head up so I could not look away. "I believe you Margrat. I do." Then he left me and went up to his study. I imagined him climbing the stairs and opening the door. I saw at once the bottle of snake root, where I had left it on the desk and the Herbal, *wiped clean, back on its shelf.*

After that things fell apart. For I was consumed now by fear of him and what he might do. At dinner that night, I sat in terror, convinced that he would poison me. He knew it and made an exaggerated play of tasting every dish of food and glass of wine. He read to me from The Duchess of Malfi, *a play about murder, ambition, blood and lust. But I would not dance with him now.*

"You cannot make me do anything, I do not belong to you," I said, though I was trembling.

"Not yet Margrat," he said, standing close behind my chair and leaning forward to whisper in my ear. "Not yet."

That night I locked my bedchamber door and I took my chair and wedged it tight under the doorknob. I prayed fervently to God for forgiveness for what I had done and I asked him what I should do now.

∽♌♋∾

The next morning, when Martha came to me and said I was to get dressed in my best clothes, for Nicholas was taking me out, I thought quickly. I could refuse to go and he might be forced to drag me kicking and screaming from the house. Or I could go willingly and then pray I might escape. I tucked my three half crowns in my pocket and got dressed. I thought of Christophe.

With only a few now dying of the plague, the streets were crowded again. Our carriage moved at walking pace along the Strand, up Fleet Street and back into the city by way of the Ludgate. I held tight to the leather strap that hung from the roof, for the roads were rutted and riddled with potholes. Nicholas seemed not to notice and was silent the whole way, lost somewhere inside himself.

When the coach stopped at last in Duke Place and he lifted me down, he took my face in both his hands and said, "You will see in time that everything I do is for the ultimate good of all and I will be forgiven. It is meant to be, Margrat, and you cannot stop it now."

At first I did not comprehend what we were doing here, but then I saw that we had stopped near St James's, a church well known to those who planned to make a hasty marriage.

"You are wrong," I said shaking my head. "The parson will not marry us, for it would be against my will and a capital offence."

"He will, for it is all arranged. He has been well paid and after we are married you will never escape or bear witness against me."

Then, though I struggled and scratched at his face, he forced me into the church and locked the door and pocketed the key. We were halfway up the aisle and I was kicking and screaming at the sight of the parson waiting at the altar, when I felt Nicholas loosen his grip on me and I fell, cracking my elbow on the stone floor. The red mist of pain left me blind for a moment, but when it cleared, I could see that Nicholas lay unconscious on the floor beside me, blood trickling from a cut deep above his left eye.

Then Christophe was there, a hank of rope slung across his chest like a bandolier. And he was dragging me up and pulling me away towards the church door and there was no one yet to stop us. The parson had disappeared.

"The door is locked." I cried out, "Nicholas has the key in his pocket."

Christophe stopped, let go of me and went back to where Nicholas lay. He rolled him onto his back and started to search his pockets. But just as I thought Christophe would find the key, there was a cry and Nicholas was come to and had grabbed Christophe's wrist tight. I ran back and snatched at Nicholas's hair and pulled as hard as I might and he cried out with pain and let go of Christophe's wrist. And in an instant Christophe had my hand and we were running towards a door to the back and side of the church, our footsteps

*echoing loud and Nicholas in pursuit. Through the door
we went and were at the bottom of the church's tower.
Up, up, up the steps and out onto the lead of the church
roof. And Nicholas coming after us.*

*Fear gripped my throat so tight I could hardly
speak, but the sound of his feet on the stone stairs, swift
and terrible, spurred me on, though I did not see now
how we would escape him. Hand in hand, Christophe
and I scrabbled and slid our way down the roof until at
last we were on the edge. The houses were huddled close
around the church, their roofs nearly touching its walls.
Christophe slipped the hank of rope from over his head
and tying one end around the steeple, he tossed the coil
of rope over the side of the tower. We watched the rope
uncoil until it reached the ground. It was a very long
way down. Christophe looked into my eyes and held my
hand and squeezed it. I knew what he wanted me to do,
but fear rooted me to the spot. Even though
I could hear that Nicholas was nearly upon us. A few
steps more, a heartbeat closer.*

"I cannot climb down the rope," I whispered.

*"You must, for if the Doctor finds the casket, then
you hold the key."*

*"No, no, for he has the casket already and my ring
will not open it."*

"*I do not understand. I thought you were the red-haired maiden... the true...*" *He gasped. Blood drained from his face. "Dieu... now I understand what it means. Do you carry a child inside you... a daughter,* his *daughter?"*

My hand instinctively felt for the imperceptible swell of my belly. Though he had told me before, now I had to face the truth of what he was saying. If the baby I carried was a girl... and had red hair... then I knew what would come to pass. Nicholas would take her from me and, when she was 14, he would use her to open the casket. The horror of it, as burning and hot as I imagined the fires of hell. Oh, yes, I must escape now, or die trying. But just as I leaned forward and prepared to grab hold of the rope, I was pulled back and felt the cold press of steel against my throat. The blade whispered across my neck as if it caressed it. Christophe cried out in desperation, but there was nothing he could do. A step closer and Nicholas would slit my throat. But he could escape... and be free to help me still.

Nicholas was growing impatient. "Are you waiting to see her die?" The blade pressed closer now and drew blood. I felt it trickle, warm, down my neck.

"Go," I whispered.

I thought Christophe hesitated, turning and turning

the ring on his finger. Then he slipped over the edge of the roof and was gone from sight. Still holding the knife to my neck, Nicholas dragged me across and we both looked down. I thought I would see Christophe's body spread out on the cobbles below, but I had forgotten that he had no fear of heights and was as agile as a cat. His feet pressed against the stone of the tower and hand over hand on the rope, he climbed down. Nicholas took his knife from my throat now and I could not stop him as he used it to cut the rope. But he was too late. Christophe had reached the ground safely. Pausing only for the briefest of moments to look up, he ran towards the river. God willing, he would be safe.

Nicholas put away his knife and I turned towards him and was drawn back in. His hand brushed my cheek and the diamond of his ring raised a red weal upon it. Then all went black and it felt as if the heavens trembled and the earth stood still.

৽ৡৎ ৡৎ

Nicholas has turned Martha out of the house now and he watches me like a hawk. He taunts me, saying I should not expect to be rescued a second time, for the rope-walker will never get close enough again. I know

I must escape or, if I cannot, then I must take my own life, and I do not know if I have the courage for that.

I devise a plan. At night I can hear him. He never seems to sleep. He paces up and down, up and down outside my bedchamber. He has become desperate that this child I carry should be a daughter and have my red hair. I open the door to him before he breaks it down and I find him on his knees, rocking backwards and forwards, backwards and forwards, weeping. A chink in his armour. A weakness exposed. Now I know how it is I must play my card, the queen. I take him back into my bed. And every night after that, though he is always gone before dawn.

Chapter 10

He wouldn't let Claire go. Now he had her by both wrists. "Such selfishness. Margrat only thought of herself. If only I had unlocked the 21st spell, there would be Heaven now, here on Earth. My mother and my father, raised from the dead, would be at my side. You cannot understand what it is like never to have known your parents. To be raised in a supposed house of God by women who believed every flicker of humanity I showed was a sign of the Devil and needed to be beaten out of me. To have no one in the whole world who loves you and who cares whether you live or die. Can you imagine that?"

She felt tears welling up and spilling down her cheeks. She wanted her mum and dad so badly it was like a pair of giant hands had taken her heart and were squeezing the life out of it.

"But I found you at last, your birthday is over

and now you can open the casket for me. Release the spell."

Claire was frantically trying to break free, kicking out at him. But he was so much stronger than she was. He twisted her round and, with her arms pinned to her sides now, he pulled her in, his mouth resting close to her ear.

"Oh, I will have it, Claire, because unless I do, your brother will be stillborn, just like all the others."

"What are you talking about? I don't have a brother..."

"Didn't you *know*? Your mother is pregnant."

No. It couldn't be true, but then she thought about her mum's mood swings, her sickness. He was right. Why hadn't she seen it before? Why hadn't her mum said anything? And what about her dad? Did he know?

"Claire. Open the Emerald Casket for me. Save your brother's life and who knows, maybe what happens after will bring your parents together again. You want that, don't you? More than anything."

Yes. Oh yes, she did want that. "Do you promise me the baby won't die?"

"Trust me."

She felt him smile and his hold on her almost imperceptibly loosen. But she *wanted* her dad to come home because he wanted to and not because there was a baby. That wouldn't be right, would it? That wouldn't ever work. And anyway, the moment she unlocked the Emerald Casket, the little power she had over Robert would be lost. He wouldn't keep his promise. He wouldn't save her unborn brother. He wouldn't need to.

Claire turned, Robert's arms still encircling her. She looked up at him. Saw how his eyes glittered and felt his whole body tense in anticipation. Then, without a word, she brought her knee up hard into his groin. As he writhed in agony, she took her chance and ran for the door. But with a cry of rage he was after her. So close, one more step and he would catch her. In blind panic, she ran into the bathroom and slamming the door shut, she turned the key and felt for the light pull. Now she could see the window. She pushed it open wide and looked out. It was a long drop. She rubbed the palms of her hands together. They were slippery with sweat. She started to climb up onto the window ledge, one foot on the edge of the bath and a hand pushing up from the basin. But her arms and legs were trembling and she felt weak with fear.

Now there was a rhythmic crashing against the door as he put his shoulder to it and tried to break it down. She could hear the grunting, rasping sound as he flung himself repeatedly against it. Claire's mind was blanking out in terror. An animal instinct was telling her to get down and curl up, small as she could, in the little space between the bath and the basin. Wait for him to break down the door and then she would die and it would be finished. But a fierce, determined spark of anger flared up in the darkness of the terror and she made one last effort to climb up onto the window ledge. As she brought her right leg up, she felt her phone vibrating in her back pocket. " Zac, help me!" she screamed into it. "Robert's going to kill me! He's breaking down the door. A house on the Strand. No... no... the riverside. It's called..." she scrabbled in desperation to remember, "Darke House. It's called Darke House and there's steps and Egyptian figures... and oh... his car outside. Silver. Grey leather seats. Call the police. Call them! Oh, my God." She was sobbing as she slid down the wall, but then her hand made contact with something hard. She looked down. Spray cleaner. She listened as the wood splintered and cracked. Felt calmer now. Steadied her breath. As he came crashing through the door, she was ready for him. Held the cleaner in her hand and sprayed him straight in the eyes. He roared in pain and stumbled, reaching out for the basin and blindly turning on the taps. Splashing the water into his eyes in desperation to wash out the burning liquid.

Claire pushed past him and ran. Along the landing all in darkness. Stumbling down the great oak stairs. But still too many steps from the front door when she heard him behind her. No time to get out now, so she slipped into the carved wooden cupboard, where his coats were kept, and pulled the door in silently behind her. Hoping he wouldn't find her. Knowing he would. Though sound was muffled inside, she could feel him getting closer and her nose was filled with the sweet, unsettling smell of him. Cassia, myrrh, aloes. Cinnamon and flowers. Then the whispering, soft and insistent. *Claire. Claire.* As if he was trying to draw out her soul.

I won't listen. I won't listen. I won't listen.

But though she pressed her palms hard against her ears, the words still repeated, filling up her head.

Then the door swinging open and the coats parting and his hot breath on her face and his thumbs pressing down on her windpipe. Not enough to kill her. Just enough to turn the darkness blood red. Her eyes rolled up and she began, as he intended, to slip out of consciousness. All she could hear now was a noise like the sound of the wind sighing through leaves. A soft dull thud, like a great oak felled and falling into soft earth and then the pressure on her throat was gone and there was light dazzling her eyes, and arms cradling her and a voice saying "Claire. You are okay. Please... you are okay now. The police are coming."

* * *

They'd told her later that it had taken four men to hold Robert down. She could hear him shouting out in the hall. Hear him calling her name. Raving, saying he must have the spells, she must fetch the spells or he would die.

She'd pressed her fingers into her ears, but could still hear him. She was in shock. Shaking so much her teeth were chattering, even though Zacharie had found a blanket to wrap her in and was holding her close and stroking her hair.

"I was so afraid I would not find you in time," he said. "But then, just as it does when I first step out on the wire, the fear went and I could think fast. I ran. Across the bridge and onto the Strand. I know it already. But which house? You know what? The ring showed me. I don't know how it works. It is…"

"Bee-zarr." Claire smiled.

"Yes. Amazing! As I ran one way, nothing. But as I ran the other, just as you said, the ring felt hotter and when it was so tight I thought my finger would drop off, I saw the car and looked up at the house and there were the Egyptian figures."

For a few moments, inside their heads, they both re-lived the scenes that had come after that, until Claire broke the silence.

"He said *my* ring would open the box. He'd followed me to the circus. He knew about you, Zac. I think he knew about your ring." Claire's throat was bruised and her voice was hoarse.

The ambulance men had wanted to take her to the hospital. But it wasn't the one her mum and

Micky were in, so she'd said she wouldn't go. "Please, just get my dad and he can take me home. I'm tired. Just very, very tired that's all. I'll be fine." The ambulance man had looked at Zacharie, raised his eyebrows… as if to say, "What do you think, mate?" And Zacharie had nodded and said, "She'll be okay. I'll stay." And he had pulled her in closer and she'd felt his lips press down on the top of her head.

Now, with her eyes closed and cradled against him, she told him about her grandma and her obsession with plague and with circuses. What she knew about the casket and the spell and the ring. About Robert's visits and the smell of cinnamon and flowers that hung around him like a cloud of incense. How Robert had talked of Margrat as if he had known her in life. How she, Claire, knew the name from her family tree, and the sheaf of papers bound up with the red linen braid. And finally how Robert had told her the only way she could save her unborn brother's life was to open the Emerald Casket.

Zacharie said nothing and when the silence went on for too long, Claire pulled away from him and sat up and saw that he was frowning, tiny lines forming between his eyebrows. His mouth looked set and hard. He didn't believe what she was telling him. That was it. He'd been drawn unwittingly into this madness and he didn't want any more to do with it. She couldn't blame him. He was a stranger after all. She was nothing to him... her hand, still trembling from the shock, went up to his mouth and touched it. A ghost of a smile and then he took her hand in his and held it so tight it hurt. But she didn't pull away.

"Claire, you know when we met, I told to you about some prophecy. Do you remember? Well, I thought it was stupid. A stupid fantastical *histoire* my family had made up. Jacalyn believed it though. I heard her whispering it to herself every night. On and on until I knew it by heart, too."

"What does it say will happen?"

And when he told her, she felt the puzzle was finally taking shape.

"Robert must know it too! He thinks I'm the red-haired maiden doesn't he? And he thinks I'm the true daughter. But what does *that* mean? Claire's free hand went up to touch the silver chain. "But he knew my birthday and that I was going to be 14."

"When? When is your birthday?"

She'd forgotten. With all the chaos and terror, she'd forgotten her birthday! She looked up at Zacharie, eyes wide in surprise.

"Today. My birthday's today."

* * *

A young police officer, Emma, had been left to look after them. She'd been told to stay until Claire's dad came and she hovered nervously around, putting a stop to any more talk about the prophecy, until Zacharie, flirting with her outrageously, said saving people's lives made you feel very, *very* hungry. The way they were looking at each other made Claire feel inexplicably cross and she snapped, "Breakfast would be good!"

And Emma said, "Oh god, yes. Sorry. You *must* be starving. I'll see if there's bread for toast and make some coffee." And she rushed off.

There had been other policemen, a couple of detectives and some forensic people in the house too, but they'd gone now. Claire could hear them out on the street and then driving away. There was someone still on the front door, but only Emma in the house and she was down in the basement kitchen.

"I'm going to look for the box," Claire said, "before Emma comes back."

"I'll come with you." He slipped his hand into hers, had started to pull her towards the door, when they heard Emma call up, "Zac, I can't seem to get the gas to light…"

"You go. I'm *sure* you can keep her busy while I look."

Zacharie made a face at her. "Don't be long… or I'll start to worry." And for a second, he came so close, she thought he was going to kiss her.

* * *

She was afraid the door to Robert's study would be locked, but it was wide open and the smell of the incense, the cinnamon and flowers was so strong inside the room, she had to will herself not to be sick. She went and drew back the curtains and pushed the window open as far as it would go. Light flooded in and she breathed the cool, damp early morning air. When her breathing had steadied, she turned back into the room, ready to start searching for the box. What was it Robert had called it? The Emerald Casket. And there it was, on his desk. Waiting. Unconsciously, her left hand felt for the ring as it had begun to do when she felt afraid. It felt tight and hot. She stepped forward and pulled the box towards her. There was the sound, and getting louder, of someone calling her. She tilted the box upwards so she could see the crocodile-head cartouche clearly, and she pressed her ring into it. Words were twisting and whispering in her head, *Soon. Have patience, for the time has not yet come.*

And now someone was shaking and shaking her. "Claire! Claire!"

It took her a second to register where she was. She looked down at the box she still held in her hands. It was closed tight.

"You found it then?" Zacharie took it out of her hands and started to examine it. "It doesn't look much does it? Have you tried opening it?" He glanced at his own ring.

"Yes, and nothing happens," she said, taking the box back from him and tucking it under her arm. Zacharie was looking at her oddly... almost as if he didn't believe what she was saying. "Look," she said, rapidly changing the subject and pointing under the desk. "Robert's bag. The one he always carries around with him."

Zacharie bent down and pulled it out. Undid the buckles. Looked inside. Counted 20 small, yellowing scrolls each tied with a strip of red linen. He picked one out. "Shall I open it? What are we looking for?"

"I don't know, something… a clue." She watched Zacharie unroll it carefully and together they looked at the hieroglyphs filling the pages, the inks still vivid. Around the edge of the scrolls, a design like twisted rope. And dancing on it, a line of rope-walkers, male and female. All with red-gold hair.

"*C'est moi!*" Zacharie held out the scroll to Claire, "It's me!"

She took the scroll and looked at it. At the writing, the spell… if that's what it was… written down. "Let's open the other scrolls," she said. "I don't know, maybe one of them…"

But they all looked the same. Different combinations of hieroglyphs for sure and now she looked carefully, she could see each ropewalker had a subtly different face; its own individual character. But there were no clues she was able to decipher.

"*Zut!* Look at this one!" Zacharie held out the scroll for her to see. "See... there's the box... and it's unlocked!"

Claire snatched it from his hand. Saw at the top of the scroll a figure with the body of a man and the head of a bird with a long curved beak, holding up an open casket out of which swirled silvery blue dust and glittering stars and galaxies of light.

Claire looked down at the Emerald Casket tucked tight under her arm. She closed her eyes, tried to imagine what would happen if she could open it, but there was only a feeling of an immense power just out of reach.

She could feel Zacharie's hot breath against her neck as he leaned over her shoulder to look at the scroll again.

"Interesting. So the box *can* be opened. Maybe it's *my* ring..."

And before Claire could stop him, he'd slipped the casket from under her arm and had pressed his ring into the oval of the cartouche. She held her breath. But there was nothing... and if he heard any words whispering in *his* head… then he wasn't saying. But he looked thoughtful. "Maybe you need knowledge and power from the other scrolls first, before you can open the box."

"What?" she said sharply, snatching the casket back from him and holding it close.

Zacharie looked as though he was weighing things up. Making a calculation. She'd been going to say, "I don't think you do. It just has to be the right time." Instead she made a joke of it. "Thank God I don't have that knowledge and power then!"

"But *he* does. He has it."

"Yes, but the police have got him. They won't let him go. You saw what he was like. Insane. Dangerous."

Claire felt a momentary surge of confidence that quickly ebbed away as she saw Zacharie's expression. Saw the shrug and heard him say, "Oh, *cela arrive tout le temps*. It happens all the time. Murderers, rapists – released because of some technicality. Or because some 'psychologist' believes that they've changed. And besides, he has power. Power we can only guess at. Do you think the police will be able to hold him? Do you? Really? No, the only way you will be safe is if he is dead."

"But he's not dead is he?"

"No, but he *will* be. We can make sure of that."

* * *

"Tea! Toast!" Emma was standing at the bottom of the stairs, holding up a tray. "I've been looking for you. Oh, and Claire, I've had a message from your dad. He's on his way. He'll be here very soon."

Claire looked round at Zacharie, hesitated for a split-second, but she could feel his hand in the small of her back giving her a little push. She hitched her backpack up on her shoulder, feeling the sharp edge of the casket inside it, poking through.

"Just think what he was shouting when they took him away, Claire. That he *dies* if he doesn't have the spells. Maybe it is not enough to remember them. Maybe he has to have them in his hands. No spells. He dies. If you believe him, that is."

Claire did. "You take them," she'd whispered, thrusting Robert's bag into Zacharie's hands. "Hide them. Don't tell me where. That way I can't tell anyone else."

"Let me take the box, too. Then *you* will

be safe." Zacharie held out his hand coaxingly.

Why not give it to him? He WAS the guardian, wasn't he? And she knew HE couldn't open it. But there were the words whispering inside her head… *not yet, not yet, not yet.* So, even though Zacharie clearly thought this meant she didn't trust him, she said, "No. The box has to stay with me."

* * *

Claire's dad was looking dishevelled and unshaven and when he wrapped his arms around her to give her a hug, she could smell sleep still on him and a faint but insistent, perfume. Sharp and citrussy.

"Ugh. You're all scratchy," she said pulling back. "Come on. I want to go home now." Before her dad had a chance to say more than 'hello' and 'thanks' to Zacharie. Before he found out Zacharie was with the circus, found out how old he was and came over all heavy and moral. As if he had any right to do that. Not that it would stop him.

"Okay. Okay. Little Miss Bossy, let's go." Claire's dad looked at Zacharie and said, sounding gruff and awkward, "Thanks for saving her life. God knows…"

Zacharie held up both his hands, palms outward, "*Pah! C'est rien.* It is nothing." Smiled.

As Claire left, she turned to look at him. He made a phone sign and mouthed, "Ring you later."

* * *

By the time they left, it was rush hour. Crawling along Chelsea Bridge Road and onto Chelsea Bridge, the car was almost at a standstill. They were on their way to Grandma's house, so Claire could wash and change. Then they were going to the hospital to see her mum and Micky. There would be plenty of time to talk later, but just now she didn't feel like it. She had her arms wrapped tightly around her backpack and her head turned away from her dad. She was looking out of the window, trying to get a glimpse of the river between the stream of people hurrying past.

"This Zacharie seems a bit different." Her dad was trying to sound all jolly and upbeat. Ugh!

"What, you mean because he's *foreign*," Claire snapped.

"Well… no! Just that he seems," Claire flinched,

because she knew exactly what her dad was going to say, "older than your other friends."

"He's not a friend. He's just someone I know. At least *he* had his phone turned on. You ought to be grateful. He saved me."

"How do you know him then?"

Claire ignored the question. Carried on looking out of the window.

"Want to tell me what happened?" Her dad's hand rested briefly on her knee.

She shook her head. "No!"

Silence.

"I feel so guilty," her dad was saying. "If I'd been around…"

If you'd had your phone switched on ever. If you hadn't been too busy. If you hadn't been cheating on Mum? She knew he wanted her to say, "It's okay, Dad. It's not your fault." But she didn't feel like doing that. She let him ramble on. She registered the rise and fall of his voice. The tone breathy and sincere and a little bit earnest. As if he was an actor playing the part of a contrite father. She would still love him. He was her dad. But she would never believe in him quite as much, ever again. She didn't ask what he had been doing all the time she'd been trying to call him. She knew, but didn't want to have him say it. Besides, there were other bigger and more important things to worry about than the small everyday tragedy of a parent's infidelity, and as if he had read her mind, he said, "They won't let him out, you know. The DI said they'd got the duty psychiatrist out of bed. He'll be sectioned. No question. He's clearly a nutter. What on earth your mum thought she was doing…"

She did turn her head towards him then. Dropped the bombshell. "Yeah. Well people do strange things when they're pregnant."

* * *

Claire turned the key in the lock and pushed the door open. Her footsteps echoed in the hall. There was no other noise anywhere. No background buzz from a television or radio. No taps dripping. Even the clocks had run down and stopped. There was just chill, empty silence. Her dad was still outside. He'd said he wanted to get something out of the boot, but when she looked back he was still in the driver's seat and on the phone, dropping a bombshell now himself; saying to *her*… the sharp-faced smiling woman… "Sorry, I am SO sorry. Jill's pregnant…"

Shouldering her backpack, she went upstairs. On the landing she hesitated. She didn't want to go in to Grandma's bedroom, but the door was ajar. She pushed it further open with her foot. She felt so incredibly tired. She wanted someone to help her and there was no one. Only Zacharie would understand and he was miles away. Then like a little miracle, her phone rang.

"Yes?"

"*C'est moi*. Are you okay?"

"Yep. I'm okay now… but so tired Zac."

"Sleep. *Dors bien*. Speak tomorrow."

She crawled onto the bed. She'd shower and change in a minute, but first she just wanted to rest. She pulled the covers around her and, holding the backpack tight, fell deeply asleep.

Manuscript 10

I bide my time. I wait patiently through all the baking heat of summer, until one Sunday at the very beginning of September, Nicholas comes to tell me that a fire has started in the city. In Pudding Lane. Since everywhere is tinder dry, the fire takes hold quickly. By Monday it blazes well. It does not threaten us at first, but Nicholas is watchful.

As the fire spreads, people run about the streets distractedly. They cry out. Soon the rumour spreads that the fire has not come about by chance. Dutchmen have been seen throwing fireballs into houses. A Dutch baker is arrested and taken to Gatehouse Prison. Foreigners are dragged out into the street and beaten.

That night I take Nicholas to my bed early, while it is still light. I say that I have seen the error of my ways. That the sight of people suffering from the plague has made me question God's beneficence.

The casket must be opened. The 21st spell set free.

"Feel," I say, placing his hand on my belly. "I carry the baby higher this time, which signifies that it is a girl."

In sleep, curled against me and with his head resting so he can feel the baby stir inside me, he looks untroubled and at peace. So when, later, we are woken by a knocking at the door and a messenger from the king says that he is needed urgently at the palace, he is not afraid to leave me alone. He sends the messenger back to the king, saying he will come at once. Then he gets dressed and, taking his leather bag with him as he always does, leaves the house, saying I must not worry. He will be back as soon as he can.

Through my bedchamber window, I watch him stride away, his bag slung across his shoulder. His cane tapping on the cobbles. Then from around the corner, a crowd appears, roistering and roiling like boiling oil. They are baying for blood, looking for someone to blame for the fire. This is my chance. I break the glass in the window with a fire iron. At the sound, the mob stops and looks up. I point a finger at the figure of Nicholas, nearly out of sight in the gathering darkness. I scream "Dutch. He is Dutch. He has fired a house nearby and heads towards St Paul's!"

All at once there is an angry roar and the mob breaks into a run. Now I seize my chance. Taking a fire iron and using all my strength, I go to his study and force open the door. The wood splinters around the lock and the door springs open wide. The Emerald Casket is there on the desk, still wrapped in its cloth. I tuck it safe under my arm. Then, from its hiding place behind the wainscot in my bedchamber, I take my manuscript. In it I have written down everything that has happened since I first met Nicholas at the Frost Fair. I slip off the red linen braid that secures it. I take off my silver necklace and place it on the oak table by the window. Then I thread the ring on its old red braid and tie it around my neck. I will scrawl a note, saying I have gone from him now and will place the ring and the casket where he will never find it. Which I truly mean to do.

If by some trick of fate he escapes the mob, he will find the necklace and the note and know that I have gone from him for ever and he will never have the key and the Emerald Casket now.

Along with the three half crowns from my mother, I will leave the house. The streets are thronged with people streaming out from the city. Carts are loaded down with their goods and chattels. All is chaos and *disorder. Black smoke hangs like a pall over the city. The heat is so great in places, even the stone cracks and breaks. I pray that I will find someone passing who will be willing to take me safe out of the city. And only God knows what the future will hold, for* 'qua redit nescitis horam.' *Ye know not the hour of his coming again.*

Chapter 11

Her mum was sitting up in the hospital bed, looking very tired. Her hair was lank and she'd pushed it roughly back behind her ears. Her eyes looked red and puffy, as if she'd been crying. Claire went straight to give her a hug and then sat on the side of the bed and held her hand. Claire and her dad had agreed that they wouldn't tell her what had happened. Not yet. Not until she was better and out of hospital.

Her mum gave her a half smile, said "What HAVE you got in that backpack?" but she was already looking past Claire, to where her dad stood awkwardly at the foot of the bed. "Claire, pop down and see Micky for a bit will you? There's some things I need to talk to your dad about."

"Not now, Jill, please…."

Claire looked from one to the other. She

squeezed her mum's hand even tighter. "It's okay," she said, "I know what this is about. The baby."

"What?" Her mum looked startled and then, silently, she started to cry.

Her dad's head was bent down and he was rubbing his forehead hard with his right hand. When he glanced up Claire thought she had never seen anyone look so miserable in the whole of her life.

"You're pregnant right?" Claire said.

Claire's mum started to sob now and she reached out with her free hand to Claire's dad. Then, when he came close, she clung onto him and he held her, resting his cheek on the side of her head. Looking as if the door to the prison cell had just closed behind him and there was no hope now that he would ever be free. Then, just as it looked as if they would be locked into this terrible freezing misery for ever, a nurse appeared holding Micky by the hand.

"There you are," she said. "I told you your mum was okay. And your dad and sister are here too. Isn't that nice?"

* * *

Micky could see something was up and she was going to nag away at them until she was told what it was. So Claire told her. "Mum's pregnant."

Micky looked puzzled at first and then her face broke into a great big grin. "Brilliant. Does that mean we're going back home to live now?" Even Mum and Dad had to smile at the sheer innocent simplicity of that. "And I hope it's a boy this time, because I'd really like a brother. I think that would be much better than another *sister*." She made a face at Claire and Claire made one back.

"Well, at least *you'll* be happy, Micky," said Mum, sounding unnaturally bright, "They've done a scan and it *is* a boy." Then she reached over to the bedside cabinet and picked up a print. A blurry black-and-white image. "A miracle to be able to see him." she said. "Your grandma lost three baby boys, one after the other. They were all stillborn. Imagine the pain of that. Maybe that's why she was always so hard and difficult…"

Claire felt cold to the bone. She took the print out of her mum's hand and looked down at it. If she believed what Robert had said… and she did, her brother would die and there was nothing she could do to stop it happening.

* * *

Claire and her dad and Micky drove back from the hospital in silence. Mum would be in hospital for a few days yet, so he was taking them back to their old house. Micky had been chattering on about the baby the whole way and didn't seem to mind that no one else was saying anything. When they got home she ran straight upstairs and went into her old room, just as if nothing had happened. Soon Claire could hear her pulling out toy-boxes from under her bed. Toys her mum had said were baby toys and wouldn't take to Grandma's. Baby. Would there be a baby? Claire felt a tight pain in her chest as if her heart had shrunk very small.

She went up to her room. She didn't want to. It felt unsettling, stripped of nearly all her possessions. But it was better being out of her dad's way. They had nothing to say to each other. And the rest of the house felt different. Her dad had made changes, moved things around. Then there were the small things, like a bottle of moisturiser in the bathroom; a make her mum could never afford to use. The house smelled strange too. Different perfumes and soaps and deodorants. Another brand of washing powder scenting the towels and the sheets. And her dad was different too. He tried to act normally. So, when it was time for bed, he'd read Micky a story and he'd sat on Claire's bed and held her hand. But she could tell, in his head and heart, he was really somewhere else. And later she heard him talking for a long time on the phone. His voice a low, soft murmur. She understood what that meant now. The need to be with someone so badly. The wanting to hear their voice.

He doesn't really want us here, she thought. *He'll be relieved when Mum's out of hospital and we can go back to the other house.* How shocking that was, but she knew in her heart of hearts that she didn't belong here any more.

* * *

She lay awake, the backpack tucked safely under the covers, between her feet. She was trying to work out where she could hide the casket. Keep it safe until…

Then she must have fallen asleep, because at four o'clock in the morning, just as it was getting light, she woke up, crying. She'd been dreaming. She was in Robert's house again. But it wasn't his house. Not really. And she wasn't Claire. She was leaning out of a window and watching someone who was Robert and yet *not* him, walking away from her down the street. She could hear the tap, tap, tap of his black cane on the cobbles. He stopped and turned to look up at her. Then a crowd of people erupted into the street and gave chase and he turned and was swallowed up into blackness.

The dream clung to her and she couldn't go back to sleep again. She got up, drew back the curtains and looked down the garden, absently twisting the silver chain she was still wearing round her fingers. She'd believed him when he said it was Margrat's. She didn't think he was mad. And she knew he would come to find her.

She padded over to the bed and, sitting on the edge of it, hauled up the backpack and took out the casket. She rubbed the edge of the ring with her thumb, turning it round and round on her finger. How cool it felt now. How heavy. Then she pressed the ring into the cartouche again. But it stayed closed. Enigmatic. She listened... but there

Chapter 11

were no words this time, filling up her head. Maybe Zacharie was right after all. You did need the powers of the other spells, too.

* * *

Micky was up. She was sitting cross-legged on the floor in the living room, eyes glued to the TV, shovelling cereal into her mouth. She ignored Claire.

Her dad was in the kitchen, leaning back on the work surface, drinking coffee. "Sleep okay?" he asked.

"Bit rubbish…" she said, starting to open cupboard doors, looking for something to eat.

Then the phone went, three rings and her dad snatched it up. "Yes?" For a second he must have thought it was work, but then his face sort of screwed into a frown and he looked quickly across at Claire. "Oh for God's sake," he said to whoever was on the other end of the phone. "When? Now what do we do?" He put the phone down and then he came over and put his arms round Claire's shoulders. "They let the bastard get away. Can you believe it? How the hell did he manage *that*? What

257

is he, some sort of magician? I tell you, if anything happens, I'll…"

"Who? What are you talking about?" As if she had to ask.

"That man. Him. They were transferring him to a 'secure' psychiatric unit, and God knows how, he got away. Maybe he had outside help. But it only happened a bit ago, so it's okay. The police are going to send some men to… you know… look after us. They'll be here any minute. Then we'll be safe. And they say it won't be long before they catch him, so…"

"He knows where Grandma's house is." Claire was calculating… thinking things through in her head.

"Who?"

"Robert. He knows where Grandma's house is. We should be there not here."

"No way." Her dad was shaking his head. "It wouldn't be safe."

"But as you said, the police will look after us. And it will be over quicker. He'll come looking for me and then the police will get him. Simple. He won't be able to hurt us, not with police all over the place." Claire had to smile as she said that. She didn't believe it for one second. But at least this way there was a chance he'd be caught. The alternative was that he'd be on the loose and she would never know when he would resurface. When he would come for her. Her life wouldn't be worth living.

"Come on Dad," she said, "let's do it. But Micky has to stay out of it. She has to stay here, in your house, with Lindsay." Her mum would be furious at the thought of Micky with her dad's girlfriend. But she didn't have to know until afterwards, did she?

"Okay, if that's what you want. I'll ring the police and we'll set it up."

* * *

The minute she could, she went to her room and she rang Zacharie.

"He's escaped."

"*Merde*. That was quick. Powerful spells, huh? Are the police there now?"

"They're coming to get us. I'm going to stay at Grandma's house. My idea, because he'll know how to find me there. Thank God you've got the spells safe."

"Jacalyn would be so *angry* if she knew I had them. That the prophecy she was so obsessed with is coming true! But I think I should have the casket too, Claire. It would be safe with me. And then you would be safe too. He could never hurt you."

"Don't tell Jacalyn about the spells or the casket. Promise you won't! No one must know about them. Only us."

"Hey! I'm not *stupide*. I know how dangerous he is. I'd never risk anything happening to you. Not now."

* * *

There was what they called a 'discreet police presence' in and around the house. They hadn't wanted her there at all… said he'd probably turn up anyway without her having to act as bait. But she knew he wouldn't. She was sure he could feel when she was close… just as she felt his presence.

The house had been searched before Claire and her dad were let back in… just in case he was already in there. Post had been collected from the mat, scrutinised and then left in a pile on the hall table. It was junk mail mostly, but there was a big brown envelope with Claire's writing on it. Someone had opened it and looked inside.

"Hey," said her dad, sounding unnaturally bright and cheerful. "Something for you. That manuscript, I think. That'll cheer you up… Claire, are you okay?"

She must have gone a funny colour. She had to sit down quickly on the stairs. She put her head in between her knees, just like her mum always made her do when she felt sick.

"Look, you go up and lie down. It's late. I'll bring you some tea and something to eat then you can sleep. Your blood sugar's low. And this weather doesn't help."

It didn't. The air was heavy with static. And it was getting dark as if a storm was brewing. Claire could feel the pressure building up inside her head. And the ring was tight and hot on her finger.

"Go on. Take the envelope with you." He was hunkered down in front of her and tilted her face up, landing a sloppy great kiss on the end of her nose.

"Dad!"

He grinned, "Go on. Hop it. I'll be up in a bit."

She drew back the lace curtains in Grandma's

bedroom and sat on the bed, in the half light, propped against the pillows and with the envelope on her lap. She looked out at the darkening sky. It felt as if the air around her was cracking and fizzing. Then she watched as a flash of lightning ripped through the blanket of rolling black clouds. She counted. *One. Two. Three.* The thunder was overhead now and so loud it rattled the windows and made her teeth buzz. Another flash. The line of houses across the street were in stark relief, as if everything around them was on fire. *One. Two. Three.* The thunder was rolling away and now the rain was starting. Hailstones first, peppering the windows so hard Claire thought the glass would crack. Then great, fat raindrops, first a few and then so many they ran in great torrents down the window.

Poor policemen outside, she thought. They would be soaked to the skin. She reached across and turned on the bedside light. Then she took out the translation from the envelope and started to read. Hardly noticed when her dad brought up a cup of tea and a sandwich. The tea grew cold and the sandwich was left uneaten on the bedside chair. And when she had finished Margrat's story, Claire knew exactly what Grandma had been trying to do, with her collection of newspaper cuttings, accounts of plagues and the family tree. It all made perfect sense now. She had been trying to work out the pattern. See if she could trace *him*, Nicholas Robert Benedict, alias Robert Benoit, her grandfather eight times removed (and Claire's blood, too – how shocking was that?) down through the centuries. But she had never even come close. Could only ever pinpoint, by tracing the outbreaks of plague, a city or a country where he had been. As for the man himself, it had been like looking for a needle in a haystack. *But then I was born,* thought Claire, *with my red hair. And Grandma must have hoped that once I was old enough to wear the ring, somehow I'd act like a magnet and he'd come for me, believing that at last all the spells were within his reach. And who knows what she thought would happen then. But she must have believed that I, with her help, was destined to take the spells from him and give them back to their guardian, a rope-walker. Then he, Nicholas Robert, would be destroyed. And once he was dead, his power would be gone and no more baby boys would need to die. There would be no more wickedness. No more unnecessary grief.*

Then she'd had her heart attack and there was only me, Claire.

"I've found him, Grandma. He's still alive!" she whispered in the darkness. "And I've found the rope-walker too and his name's Zacharie and I've given him Robert's scrolls now, so they are safe. But… the casket, I've kept it and I promise I'll never let Robert have it. And I don't know how I'll do it, but I'll save my brother. I won't let him die. Cross my heart."

* * *

Days passed and there had been no visible sign of him anywhere near the house. Though someone had been in to his house on the Strand. Drawers turned out and cupboards emptied. His study had been ransacked.

There'd been sightings in Brighton, Edinburgh, New York and as far away as Buenos Aires, but Claire knew that he wasn't in any of those places. He was somewhere close by, she could feel him. Almost smell the cinnamon and flowers, hear his voice saying her name. And he'd know she had taken the spells and the casket.

"I wish he would come," she whispered to Zacharie, talking to him on her phone, late at night, in the darkness. "Then, whatever happens, it would be over and done with."

"Let me come and get the casket. All this waiting is driving me *insane*. I just need to see you. Shall I come over? I could come now!" Zacharie sounding so intense, so desperate.

"All this waiting is driving me mad too. But you mustn't come. He knows you're the Guardian. He might not risk coming if you're here. And I'm sure he's watching the house. He'll make a move soon. He will. He's going to have to. And when he does..."

But the police and her dad had started to believe the threat had receded and were beginning to relax. She could feel the tension slipping away. They thought he'd probably left the country, or was in hiding somewhere and wouldn't risk being caught. She heard her dad on the phone, making plans to get back to work. She heard him talking to Micky. Mum rang from the hospital and said they were letting her out just as soon as they were sure the baby was safe. Where there had been four policemen on duty in and around the house, now there was only one.

But she couldn't rest. This couldn't go on. The waiting. Something had to happen. But she didn't know what. *Margrat's* rope-walker would have known. She felt sure of it. But when she rang Zacharie he didn't seem to. He was as much in the dark as she was.

"You *could* ask Jacalyn, Maybe she'll be able to help." Though Claire didn't believe she would. Was relieved when Zacharie said, "She stays out of it. The ring's mine. I must deal with HIM. And I will. *Je promis*. But you have to trust me. I don't think you do, Claire… or you would give me the box."

"Of course I trust you. You saved me from Robert AND you saved me from being crushed by all those tumbling acrobats!"

"Don't joke, Claire. You must prove that you do…"

"Zacharie… Zac…"

But he'd gone. And when she tried to ring him again, it went straight to voicemail.

* * *

Dad had made pasta with tomato sauce for tea. They were balancing their plates on their knees in front of the television, watching the local London news and, because it was pretty boring stuff, Claire was only half listening. She was checking her texts obsessively. She'd heard nothing from Zacharie and it was eating her up.

Then her heart leaped. A text from him! *'Nothing is going to happen while you're safe in the house. Be at the Jubilee Gardens for the highwire walk at 8 o'clock. We need to flush Robert out into the open so we can deal with him… and bring the box with you. We might need it.'*

Maybe Zac was right after all. It was risky, scary, but nothing *would* come of doing nothing. She had to do something. So she texted straight back. *'I'll be there.'*

"Jeez! Look at this Claire." Her dad was pointing at the TV screen with his fork. "Isn't that Zacharie? The one who saved you. He says he's going to wirewalk the Thames tonight! Bloody hell… maybe *he's* delusional too. Do you think he'll make it?"

She sat up so suddenly the pasta nearly slipped off her plate. Her dad reached across and took it from her. "Careful!"

But she wasn't listening. She was leaning

forward, looking at Zacharie's face, animated, talking to camera and telling everyone what he was planning to do. "Turn it up! Turn it up!"

"Yeah, OK. Hold your horses!"

And then the presenter asked him the question "Why are you doing this now? Is it for charity or is it just a massive publicity stunt to advertise the circus?"

"Circus?! You never said he was with a circus…"

And this made her catch her breath… Zacharie turned to the camera and said very clearly, "A publicity stunt, of course. Planned for a long time… but *I do it also for Claire. So that she knows I risk my life for her…*"

"Does he *know,*" said Dad, incredulously, "that you're only 14? If I ever see him again I'll break every bone in his body. You stay clear of him Claire. Do you understand?"

Eight o'clock. Eight o'clock. He wants me to be there in just over an hour. She had to get out of the house. Right this minute. But how was she going to do that? Her dad was still fuming about Zacharie. Couldn't stop going on and on about him.

But in the event it was easy. She found the single

policeman still on duty and she asked him if he would like a cup of tea! And, not suspecting a thing, he said he would. He followed her into the kitchen where her dad was clearing up the dishes and stood around talking to him about computers and all the problems he'd been having sorting his out. And her dad was distracted and Claire was able to slip away, pick up her backpack, nip out of the French doors in the dining room, through a gap in the hedge and into next door's garden. She scrabbled over their wall and dropped down into the street beyond. Then she'd run as fast as she could to the tube station. Rummaging in the outer pocket of her backpack she found her travel card and was soon through the barrier and pushing past people down the stairs and onto the platform. She was so agitated and out of breath that people were staring at her. When the sign said that the next train via Waterloo and Charing Cross was going to be in four minutes, she swore loudly. She wanted Waterloo. Four minutes! Four minutes! An eternity. And when it did come, it was crowded and she had to push her way on. There were no seats. She had to stand and straphang, her backpack wedged between her feet. When the tube started to move, she calmed a little. She looked up at

the map and counted the stops. She tried to send
Zacharie a text. *'Five stops from Waterloo.'* But the
message sending failed. Oh well, only five stops. Not
long. It wouldn't take long. Her eyes scanned the
faces around her. It was hot. There was a smell of
too many bodies squeezed into too small a space.
Then her heart missed a beat. There it was again.
The unmistakable smell of cinnamon and flowers.
He must have followed her from the house. Been
waiting outside. She'd known it. Heat and fear made
patches of sweat appear between her shoulder
blades and under her arms. Her T-shirt was sticking
to her body. He was here, in the carriage. Close by.
But she still couldn't see him. She couldn't move.
There was nowhere to go. At every station more
people got on. The train swayed and rattled,
hurtling on towards Waterloo. Then there was a
squeal and shriek of brakes and the train was
slowing down. Last stop now. Which side was the
platform? People had turned to face the door
opposite her, so she pushed and edged her way
closer to those doors. She was first out. Then she ran
through the crowds of people on the platform, up
the escalator, banging people with her backpack.
"Sorry! Sorry!"

Up and out into the open air and she was threading her way fast through the river of people heading towards the Jubilee Gardens. She looked at her watch. Eight o'clock. Was she too late? She looked back anxiously over her shoulder, knowing he was following her. She twisted the ring round and round on her finger… *Please let me get there before he catches me…*

Now she was in the gardens and, looking up, she could see the wire, tensioned between two cranes, one on either side of the river. People had stopped and were pointing. Claire looked up. She saw someone dressed in white, balancing on the wire, walking towards her, 45 metres above the Thames. Her hand felt for the ring again. She focused her thoughts.

Then, making her start, a text appeared on her phone. Zacharie. Not him up on the wire then… even he wasn't mad enough to be texting from up there, was he? '*Allez vite! You must climb up as quick as you can, before Jacalyn gets all the way across.*'

What!? Climb up? And why did she have to get there before Jacalyn? There was no sense in it. Much safer to be on the ground. She was going to text '*No way!*'

But then she could feel Robert closing in behind

271

her. The ring was tight and hot. She took some deep breaths. Tried to still the panic rising up inside her. She was going to have to do what Zac asked. She had to trust that he knew what he was doing... because sure as hell, she didn't. So she pushed on through the crowds until she was at the base of the crane. A circle of crash barriers kept people back and security guards were stationed inside. She looked up again. Jacalyn was halfway across. Well Zacharie had been right so far. Robert HAD followed her. He must believe she had the casket and the scrolls in her backpack and was going to give them to Zacharie... or else why would she be here? He didn't know that Zac already had the scrolls. And Claire hoped that Robert's desperation to recover the spells would blind him to the fact she was leading him into danger. That if he climbed up the crane after her, he would fall into whatever trap Zac had set. Claire knew Robert had to die or she would never be free of him. But she didn't know yet how that would happen. She could see a struggle, but not who's hand would push him to his death.

As the wind off the river swirled and eddied about the crane, there it was again, the barest suspicion of a smell. Cinnamon and flowers. She started to really panic now and was afraid she wouldn't be able control it. Jacalyn still had a long way to go, but Claire had to be up there before she finished. She didn't know why that was so important, but Zacharie said she must be. *"He knows what he's doing. He knows what he's doing."* She repeated it over and over like a good luck mantra as she pushed forward, watching the security guards, trying to judge where they would move to next, where they would be looking. Then, as the one nearest to her was distracted by a small boy climbing over the barrier, she slipped through the bars and ran round to the base of the crane, only pausing to make sure her arms were threaded through both the straps of her backpack. Then she was hoisting herself up and onto the first rung of the metal ladder that ran up, 45 metres, to where the crane's arm swung out over the river. She started to climb, very quickly at first, expecting any minute that she'd be spotted and a cry would go up and she'd be brought down. But everyone's eyes seemed to be fixed on the wire-walker. A wind had started to blow and she could see Jacalyn was struggling to balance against the power of it, though the long pole she carried was still keeping her steady.

Up and up Claire climbed. She was having to force her legs to keep moving and the muscles in her arms were screaming with the effort of pulling her body up. And the wind as she climbed higher was catching on her backpack and buffeting her about. She was terrified that she wouldn't be able to make it. That she would be stuck, clinging to the ladder, unable to move, until her grip on the ladder failed and she fell into the sea of people below. What on earth had possessed her? Why was it she hadn't stayed on the ground and made Zacharie come to her? She knew why. She looked down. A small black shape was climbing inexorably up towards her. Robert wouldn't reach her before she got to the top, would he? He was tired and his powers must be ebbing away, because he no longer had the spells that would renew them. But her arms and legs, as she pushed herself to climb on up, were starting to tremble. They were weakening with the effort, too. The ring on her finger was so tight and hot she could hardly bear it. 20 more rungs up on the ladder and Robert was starting to close the gap.

Claire was nearly at the top. Only ten more rungs to go, though Robert was so close now, she swore she could feel the heat of his body, hear the rasping of his breath above the wind. But Zacharie was there waiting for her, looking down, and holding out his hand, ready to help her with the last few steps. He pulled her to safety. As he straightened up, sweat glistening on his forehead and darkening his hair, they were face to face and she saw his eyes widen and a smile of relief flicker across his face. "You did it!"

There was a groan and a thud behind her and she turned to see Robert's hand grasping the top rung of the ladder, the diamond in the ring on his finger catching the light.

"Claire, get behind me!" And then Zacharie leaped forward and stamped down hard, on Robert's hand. It was ruthless. Efficient. Shocking. There was a cracking sound and a scream of rage and pain.

"See? I will do anything to keep you safe." Zacharie was looking back at her, with an expression of such utter determination on his face, he was barely recognisable. His beautiful mouth was twisted and his eyes were dark glittering slits. But she had to trust him. He'd saved her from Robert before. And he *was* the rope-walker, wasn't he?

"*Now* you must give me the box. Give it to me. Then I will have *all* the spells." Claire could see that he had Robert's black bag slung over his shoulder. "Quick, before he reaches you."

"Oh Claire." Robert, ashen-faced, had pulled himself up at last onto the platform and was standing looking at her. His dark hair, threaded with grey now, and his black jacket billowing out in the wind. Then he looked across at Zacharie and Claire could see that he'd registered the black leather bag. *His* bag.

Claire sensed Zacharie moving in close behind her. She reached back for his hand. Felt his strong, hard fingers close around hers and said, "Zacharie is the guardian. He'll help me just as Christophe helped Margrat. But this time *you* will die!"

The ghost of a smile lit up Robert's face, "Zacharie won't help you. *He* only wants to help himself. Don't you Zacharie? I see he has *my* spells already and now he wants the casket. He knows how valuable the spells and casket are to me… and he knows that I have money."

"Don't listen to him Claire." Zacharie's fingers were crushing hers tight. His head bent close to hers. She could feel his hot breath whispering in her ear.

"Well perhaps he wouldn't sell them. But when was it that you first thought of taking the spells for yourself, Zacharie? Of opening the casket if you could? When you came to my house and saved Claire?"

Zacharie let go of her fingers, but then his arms came up around her... too tight to reassure. But not threatening. Yet. She wanted to lean back against him, feel the strength of his body flow into hers. She badly needed to trust him... because if she couldn't, then who was there?

"But first you have to get Claire to give you the casket. Then what? Only *Claire* can open it with her ring. She is the key. So you would need Claire too... and what wicked things would you have to do to her, to make her open it?"

"Supposing I *did* sell you the spells..." Zacharie said. Claire tried desperately to twist round so she could look up at Zac's face, but he was holding her too tight. "Then what? How would you make Claire open the casket, Robert? Could you force her to do it? She wouldn't do it willingly for you either."

"For her own flesh and blood?" Robert was stepping towards them, slowly but with a terrifying determination. "You look shocked Zacharie. Didn't you know… Claire is my grandaughter ten times removed."

Claire lifted her head. "So?"

"Claire, I must have the spells or I will die. Will you watch me die?"

"Yes, then my brother will be safe."

Slowly, steadily, little by little, Claire could feel Zacharie pulling her back with him. Tiny incremental steps. His grip had tightened on her and she could feel him tense; ready to spring away from Robert. But suddenly the roar of the crowd made him stop. She could feel his body twist round as he looked over his shoulder towards his sister, safe on the platform now, stepping out of her harness and unclipping her safety wire. A pause. Then in one short, sinuous movement, Zacharie had seized Claire's wrist and was pulling her across the platform, straight towards Jacalyn. For a second Claire felt relief flood through her. Three against one. Strength in numbers. They would defeat Robert together. But then Jacalyn said, her voice calm and sure, "I won't let you do it Zacharie. You are a guardian. I won't let you betray the trust."

"And who's going to stop me? Do you think

he can? Look at him… he's finished."

Robert could barely stand now. His body swayed in the wind. His face so white, the skin looked like a mask, with black holes for his eyes and mouth.

"I will." Jacalyn's eyes glittered. Her hands clenched tight, her body tensed and ready.

"But you don't have the ring. And you never will, not while there is breath in my body. This is my chance to escape…get away from you and the circus and my suffocating life. I *will* kill you, Jacalyn, if you try and stop me."

"Zacharie!" Claire was tugging at his hand, trying to pull him back. "That's a wicked thing to say. She's your sister!"

"So? Let me see… total freedom and unbelievable power weighed against the life of just one person. Which do you think I will choose?"

Claire felt cold to the bone as she looked at his face, his beautiful mouth made ugly by the words he was saying. Was struck quite dumb as he raised his hand and brought it down hard across the side of his sister's head, knocking her off her feet. Jacalyn crashed against the railing and blood began to trickle down her face.

Then Zacharie dragged Claire past her, until they were at the very edge of the platform. Still holding Claire's arm tight, he held out Jacalyn's safety harness and told her to put it on. Zacharie was impatient, angry. Watching Claire, but also watching Jacalyn and Robert. "Now!"

Claire felt the cold sweat of fear. What was he going to make her do? She looked down over the edge of the platform, at the dark water of the river and the eddying mass of people lining its bank. Talking to herself all the while, because it made the terror manageable. "You stupid, stupid, stupid girl. Margrat was right. Just because someone looks beautiful…"

But she could see that *Zacharie* was calculating too, trying to work out how to put on his own safety harness, without letting her go. Would there be enough time? Would Jacalyn get to them first? Or would Robert?

A fleeting moment of indecision, then he let go of her, stepped into the harness and slung the black leather bag back over his shoulder. He turned to take Claire's hand, and at that moment, Robert made his move. He knew now that Zacharie had the 20 spells and planned to escape along the wire with them. Then the spells would be out of his grasp, and Robert knew that without them he *would* die. Claire watched as he gathered the last of his strength and made a desperate leap towards Zacharie, slashing his diamond ring down Zacharie's cheek.

Zacharie cried out, stumbled and his right foot stepped back off the platform. He would have fallen then, but Robert, oblivious now to the pain in his crushed hand, reached out and held onto him by the strap of the black leather bag. Once he had firm hold on the strap, he pulled it from Zacharie's shoulder and with his right foot pushed Zacharie backwards and watched as he fell. Felt the judder through the steel of the platform as the safety line broke Zacharie's fall. Watched for a second as slowly, painfully, hand over hand, Zacharie began to pull himself back up.

Robert, the black bag safely strapped across his body now, turned back to Claire. He had the 20 spells and now he wanted the Emerald Casket. And Claire would have run, tried to climb back down the ladder and escape, but Jacalyn stood in her way. "You must open the Emerald Casket now," she said, "and you must hurry."

"But that's what *he* wants me to do. And I've tried to open it and…"

" You must do it. The time of the prophecy has come. Thoth will speak and the wicked will be punished."

Claire hesitated. "*Now*," the voice in her head was saying. "*Do it now*." She hurriedly slipped off the backpack and pulled out the casket. She fitted the ring (so tight and hot the pain was almost unbearable) into the cartouche. She could feel Jacalyn standing close, her hand resting on Claire's shoulder. Saw Zacharie haul himself back up onto the platform.

But he was too late, for this time the box *was* opening. There was no scroll inside, but a silvery blue dust was spiralling up and out, forming a cloud that blocked out all light. The air became ice cold and filled with a noise, a susurration like a billion locusts on the wing. Then a few pinpricks of light appeared, then more and more until the darkness was lit by great galaxies of light, swirling together until they became one single vortex of brightness. And she felt as if she was being sucked down into it. Peace. The briefest moment of total beatitude and cradling warmth. A voice softly whispering,

"*The time* is *now.*" Hieroglyphics flashed across her mind's eye like words on a reel of tickertape. Exhilaration. A feeling of immense power charging up every atom in her body until she fizzled and crackled and was on fire with it. Now she was spinning faster and faster, gathering the silvery blue dust to her, sucking it in, compressing it down inside her until it became a dark mass of pure energy. Then she breathed out. There was a shrieking, howling hurricane of noise. The blue dust that poured from her mouth forming a tornado that swirled out from her, faster and faster. She saw Zacharie's eyes widen in fear and panic as the glittering blue tornado hit and he scrabbled to keep his hold on the railing. Then there was silence so loud, for a moment Claire was deafened by it. And empty space where Zacharie had been. And the casket was closed and locked again. And the only sound was of Jacalyn crying.

"She made a hard choice."

Robert's voice! She spun round and her face must have looked so shocked, he actually laughed.

"I know… I'm surprised too. Why wasn't I swept away? To what purpose?" And he stepped towards her, his face shining and glorious as an angel.

Claire backed away from him, wrapping her arms tight around the casket. Out of the corner of her eye she could see that Jacalyn was already alert to the danger. Was still crouched down near the railing, but was tensed and ready. Robert moved on towards Claire saying, "Give me the casket, Claire. Thoth means me to have it or I would surely have died with Zacharie." His confidence was so great that he believed that if he asked, Claire would just give him the casket. It must be clear to her now that *he* was the chosen one.

Claire's back was pressed into the railing. She had nowhere else to go. Robert's hands were on the casket. He was pulling it away from her and she was struggling to hold on to it. His foot came up and pushed hard into her thigh and with one final pull, he had the casket. Was so triumphant at that moment that he did not register Jacalyn behind him or feel the loop of steel from a safety wire around his neck, until it was too late. She was much shorter than he was and so much lighter, but she pulled down with all her weight and it was enough for him to start choking... and reach up with one hand to try and loosen the wire. Even now he wouldn't let go of the casket. Jacalyn wasn't strong enough on her own... but with Claire's help, they pulled and scrabbled and dragged Robert to the edge of the platform, to the gap where the high wire stretched out over the Thames.

"Get... the... casket." Jacalyn's grip on the safety wire was weakening and as she let go of it, Robert lost his balance and his grip on the casket loosened. And Claire was able to snatch it from him. For a split-second their eyes met and she saw herself reflected small in them. Then he was falling back through the gap, whirling round and down towards the river, his arms outstretched. And soon he had disappeared from sight into the gathering dusk.

At first Claire and Jacalyn just stood there, looking down, unable to move. And then Jacalyn's arms were around Claire and the casket... pulling them both in. And Claire buried her head in Jacalyn's shoulder and now she was safe, she began to cry.

"I followed you. Did you know?" Claire looked up at Jacalyn in surprise. "*Everywhere* that you went after we met at the circus. I didn't have the ring to help me, but I needed to know where you lived and what was happening and that you were okay.

Pah… that was exhausting! But I never trusted that Zac would help you. Never. That's a terrible thing to say of your own flesh and blood, isn't it?"

Claire was thinking of Robert. He was her flesh and blood wasn't he? And she hadn't tried to stop him falling either. She'd have to think about that later… when she was alone and the world had stopped wildly spinning.

"But my brother never *really* believed in the prophecy. At least not until the end. All Zac ever wanted was to get away from the circus and from me. You know, I never once thought *he* would die when the casket opened. I was sure that if anything bad were to happen, it would be to Robert." Now Jacalyn was crying and it was Claire's turn to comfort her.

"But Robert *is* dead too, isn't he? He must be. So it's over now and we're safe. Everyone is safe and we have the casket." She gave a sigh, thinking of her mum and Micky and her unborn baby brother. And as she breathed out, a swirl of silvery blue dust glimmered softly, just for a moment, in the dark night air.

Epilogue

They never found Robert or the black leather bag. But Zacharie's body was found much later, downstream in the river. And he was still wearing the ring. After Jacalyn had identified him, she was allowed to take it. She slipped it on to the third finger of her right hand. And it fitted perfectly.

Papers reported 'a freak weather event', a tornado of swirling blue dust, occurring at dusk, over the river. And they reported the death of Zacharie. Jacalyn told them that her brother had just stepped out on the wire when the storm had blown up out of nowhere. He'd fallen and been ripped from his safety wire by the wind, like a leaf torn from a tree. But there was no mention of a Robert Benoit. He might never have existed.

As for Claire, she melted away into the crowds the moment they reached the ground.

Claire keeps Zacharie's number on her phone. A sort of cruel memento. A reminder that nothing is ever what it seems and you must be careful who you trust, always. And she keeps Margrat's papers and their translation, tied together with the red linen braid. She will put them somewhere safe, along with the silver necklace, a copy of the family tree and the Emerald Casket. Because, although she believes that Robert must be dead, she still feels uneasy. His body and his black bag were never found, but his face as he fell still haunts her dreams. And she knows somehow the spell is now part of her… and might one day resurface, bringing fear and wickedness in its wake.

She wears the ring, as she must, for only death can part her from it. But she knows that Jacalyn will come if she, Claire, should ever need her. For the guardian's ring is Jacalyn's now. And at least the epidemic of bird flu has burned itself out; the black rats disappearing as quickly as they came. And best of all, she has a new baby brother. Matthew. Proof surely that Robert's power has failed.

Her mum and dad still live apart, but her dad was there when Matthew was born. And he calls round nearly every day and he phones now when he is away. Maybe, as Margrat believed, there is always hope. And who knows what the future will hold. But Claire is going to write her own account of what happened and put it with Margrat's, as a true record and as a warning. For as Margrat wrote, *Qua redit nescitist horam*? Who can know the hour of his coming again?

Historical Note

Just like Margrat, Samuel Pepys, the famous 17th-century diarist, also went to see a mummy 'with all its hieroglyphics', on show at the Head and Combe in the Strand. There was a brisk trade in, and a fascination with, Egyptian artefacts during this period. Mummies, for instance, were believed to have magical power and were often ground up and used as medicine (mummia).

In the 17th century many people believed that 'hieroglyphics' were secret signs – a code that, once broken, would reveal the secrets of the Universe. There was also a widespread belief in a collection of texts called *The Hermetica*. It was said to be the teachings of Hermes Trismegistus (the merging of the Greek god Hermes and the Egyptian god Thoth) and was mostly written in Egypt between the first and fourth centuries AD. But it continued to have new text added to it, including the Emerald Tablet.

It is these texts, these magical 'spells' that the Doctor finds and manages to translate from the Egyptian; the Emerald Tablet becomes, in the novel, the Emerald Casket.

The terrible powers of the Egyptian goddess Sekhmet were believed to cause epidemics and plagues. But she was also the goddess for physicians and healers, and so, was seen as being responsible for both the sickness and the cure!

The Doctor's character shows similar ambiguity. He carries a silver-topped cane and wears a diamond ring, just as – according to the popular mythology of the time – the Devil was said to do when he was seen strolling down the Strand. But, the Doctor *also* smells of cassia, myrrh and aloes, which are said to have been part of a holy anointing oil used to perfume the robes of Jesus.

The streets mentioned in the Manuscript sections of the story are largely still there and the names are recognisable, and there was a grand house of the period, since demolished, recorded as being decorated with Egyptian scenes.

The poisons mentioned and their symptoms

are accurate and would have been available at the time. Laudanum was invented in the early part of the 17th century and was in use then.

The name Benoit is a form of the name Benedict. So Nicholas Robert Benedict becomes Robert Benoit.

As to the rope-walker... there were French jugglers and rope-walkers in London at the time of the Great Plague. Foreigners were widely blamed for the sickness. Margrat's descriptions of the punishments meted out to foreigners come from eye-witness accounts.

The modern-day rope-walker is, of course, very loosely based on the French wire-walkers who crossed the Thames to Jubilee Gardens, on a wire stretched between two cranes, as part of the first Festival of the Thames, in 1997. Oh, and the prophecy is a loose mix of the biblical, with a dash of Sybilline oracle!

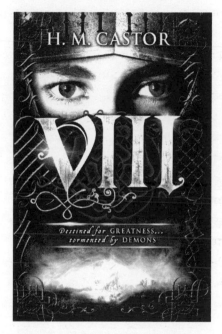